Driving the King

"Ravi Howard tells a thoroughly convincing story about the singing star Nat King Cole's best friend. . . . [A] warmly enveloping book. . . . Appealing."
—Janet Maslin, *New York Times*

"A moving tale about bigotry and the power of friendship." —*People*

"Excellent . . . moving. . . . Weary is a marvelous character who never becomes didactic. His voice is painstakingly real, precise, and authentic, allowing the reader to drop into the moment as though sitting next to him in the front passenger seat of Cole's Cadillac limousine. . . . What Howard does so well . . . is to develop a storytelling perspective out of the limelight, that of someone who is not a leader, but a follower with practical concerns of family, occupation, and personal safety. . . . Readers who appreciate beautifully written, compelling novels with great depth and humanity will be more than pleased." —*Philadelphia Inquirer*

"Heartbreaking. . . . A bold reimagining of [the] civil rights era. . . . Howard's choices . . . are daring." —*Los Angeles Times*

"By following Howard's characters, we are allowed a sidelong but penetrating glimpse into one of the most important events in American history. . . . Howard bends history . . . proving that the past can be best felt through refracted light rather than under the harsh glare of historical fact." —*Minneapolis Star Tribune*

"In an easygoing style, with Weary as his guide, Howard pokes into under-viewed corners of the fight while never losing sight of the humanity of both the cause and its effects." —*Milwaukee Journal Sentinel*

"Howard brings readers back in time to postwar Alabama, in this velvety smooth fictional memoir. . . . This story about a strong man, living with his head held high, is set against the backdrop of Jim Crow and the Montgomery bus boycott. Howard's prose goes down like the top-shelf whiskey that Weary favors, making for a heady reading experience." —*Publishers Weekly* (starred review)

"Through unfussy language and well-formed characters . . . gifted novelist Howard . . . takes readers of all races, ages, and classes into the world of pre–civil rights era black people, offering insight on and understanding of one of our country's most tumultuous periods." —*BookPage*

"Alternating between the cities and Weary's past and present, Howard explores race relations in the pre–civil rights era and the strong ties forged between two extraordinary men." —*Booklist*

"Powerful. . . . A personal, poignant portrayal of how the lives of African Americans could be so easily derailed by racial inequality."
—*Library Journal* (starred review)

"It is a beautifully wrought, 'quiet' novel and deserves a wide readership."
—*Tuscaloosa News*

PRAISE FOR

Like Trees, Walking

"Howard has a fine eye for detail and knows how to turn a good phrase. . . . Beautiful passages . . . are often interspersed with sometimes clinical and graphic description. . . . Howard is a talent to watch, and this work introduces us to a fictional universe that we'll definitely want to encounter again."
—*Washington Post Book World*

"The verdict: A breathtaking debut." —*Atlanta Journal-Constitution*

"In his stirring debut novel, *Like Trees, Walking*, Ravi Howard mines the explosive aftermath of one of America's last recorded lynchings. . . . Graced with an acute sense of his characters' lives and times, Howard reveals how racial hatred and the impulse to seek retribution must give way to redemption before one can truly break free from past injustice." —*Elle*

"[An] imaginative rendering of one of the most brutal forms of torture in American history . . . Howard reveals, in lilting and haunting prose, the intricacies of caring for the dead. . . . *Like Trees, Walking* delves into this and other questions, taking us to a historical moment when African Americans could encounter death for daring to be themselves." —*Charlotte Observer*

DRIVING *the* KING

Also by Ravi Howard

Like Trees, Walking

DRIVING *the* KING

A NOVEL

Ravi Howard

HARPER  PERENNIAL

NEW YORK • LONDON • TORONTO • SYDNEY • NEW DELHI • AUCKLAND

HARPER ● PERENNIAL

A hardcover edition of this book was published in 2015 by HarperCollins Publishers.

HarperCollins books may be purchased for educational, business, or sales promotional use. For information, please e-mail the Special Markets Department at SPsales@harpercollins.com.

FIRST HARPER PERENNIAL EDITION PUBLISHED 2016.

Library of Congress Cataloging-in-Publication Data

Howard, Ravi
 Driving the king : a novel / Ravi Howard. — First edition.
   pages cm
   ISBN 978-0-06-052961-1 (hardback) — ISBN 978-0-06-052962-8 (paperback) — ISBN 978-0-06-219915-7 (ebook) 1. Chauffeurs—Fiction. 2. Race relations—United States—Fiction. 3. Race discrimination—United States—Fiction. 4. African Americans—Social conditions—20th century—Fiction. I. Title.
 PS3608.O93D75 2015
 813'.6—dc23
                                                          2014015054

ISBN 978-0-06-052962-8 (pbk.)

16   17   18   19   20   OV/RRD   10 9 8 7 6 5 4 3 2 1

For Laura, Ellis, and Cole

The art of fiction is an art of make-believe.

—Albert Murray, *The Hero and the Blues*

DRIVING *the* KING

Chapter 1

Montgomery, Alabama

DAY OF THE SHOW
11:40 A.M.

The inbound plane was too far to see, but it would arrive on time. The desk clerk at the Centennial Hotel had called Eastern Airlines for me, and the operator said the flight had left Midway on schedule. I worried about that snow Chicago folks talk about, Lake Michigan spinning up its own kind of winter and airlines canceling flights on account of it. A clear sky was a sign that my plan might work after all. Time and weather had been kind, and the flight had surely crossed the Tennessee line by then, coming south over Alabama. In twenty minutes, Nat Cole would be on the ground in Montgomery.

I found a parking spot in the row of hired cars, just across the tree line from the rental lot. The sedans and trees had the same holiday colors—pearl and candy red on the Christmas bows and paint jobs. Garland did for the bare branches what chrome did for the fenders and the grilles. All the new models were built low, like they'd been stepped on. Seemed like everything was made with rocket ship lines, like a Ford or a Spitfire might get launched into space and take a trip around the world.

The airport was built low just like the cars parked in front. In the year I'd been gone, that stretch of country pasture had been cleared and paved, and a brand-new terminal had been built, futuristic, or somebody's best guess at what the future might look like. Concrete awnings and steel-framed windows. Red clay had settled on the base, and a good bit still caked the grout of the low bricks. It was a young, new place that looked as much planted in the ground as it did built.

As new as the place was, the line of hired cars told me I was in the same old Montgomery. My Packard fit right in with the older rides and their Negro drivers, some behind the wheel and some on the sidewalk, waiting for whoever was on that plane out of Chicago. Aside from that new airport, Montgomery's sidewalks had changed. Boycott walkers had filled them for a year. The busses looked old and empty, like the locust shells I used to find in the woods. They carried something fearsome once, but in the end, they were nothing but husks I could crush in my hand.

From what I had seen, the people enjoyed their walking. For those who didn't, a ride was easy enough to find. In the week I'd been back, I had seen many a driver pull to the curb to let walkers slide into empty seats and let the tires move for them so they could spare their feet a mile or two.

I offered a couple a ride that morning on my way to the airport. I watched them while I pulled to the side of the road. The girl had said something to make the boy laugh, but laughter or no, they were quick to glance my way, taking in the strange car slowing down on that empty stretch of Selma Highway. Maybe a year's worth of violence had taught them as much. The girl had turned a golf club into a walking stick, shiny bamboo with the iron head turned into a handle. Selma Highway had few sidewalks and enough Johnson grass for critters and snakes. That stick might come in handy if she found loose footing or creatures. There were other hazards. Some of the boycotters had been messed with, beaten. But the two of them looked in my car, saw my face, a kind black stranger with empty seats, and knew they had no reason to worry.

"Car pools don't always come this far out, so we appreciate you stopping," she said.

He tipped that apple cap at me and then to the young lady as he held the door for her. Seemed they were sweet on each other. I could tell by the way they said thank you and you're welcome with nods and eyes, nary a word.

The young man was on his way to the same place I was, wearing the uniform of the porters at Dannelly Field. The young woman wore the blue smock of Colonial Bakery, red-and-yellow logo just like the bread wrappers. They had the jobs that required first names stitched onto their chests, but I asked them all the same, introduced myself properly. With that the three of us headed down Selma Highway, Yvette Haynes, Claude Washington, and me. When they called me Mr. Weary, I told them Nathaniel was just fine.

Yvette folded her sweater into her canvas bag, and took out an apron wrapped in plastic. Half of Montgomery walked with their work whites wrapped up or folded inside out to keep them clean through all that traveling. Every season brought a different kind of road dust—pollen, red dirt, mud, crushed leaves. The boycott was a new kind of season, and it had brought problems besides the dust and the weather. The covered clothes were a shield for Yvette as much as that bamboo was her sword.

"They throw things at us sometimes, Mr. Weary. I can't show up at work looking any old kind of way if and when they do."

Her apron was bleached clean, but the satchel carried the smell of vanilla and cinnamon. Every piece of Christmas sweets Colonial made had a little nutmeg, and that canvas had some of the scent, too. The car smelled a little more like Yuletide, which was as much the season as it was the boycott's anniversary.

"Me. I'm fine walking. Did me some good. Got back down to my playing weight," Claude said. "I was all-county everything at Carver High School. Shortstop. Point guard. Free safety. I believe I told Yvette that. She might have seen me when we used to run all over her boys at Booker T."

He said as much, resting his arms on the front seat, putting on like she wasn't right next to him.

"I believe you reminded me a few times. Didn't give me enough time to forget."

When we got to the Colonial gates, Yvette thanked me for the ride and told Claude she'd see him that afternoon. After he let her out, he was about to get in the front seat before I stopped him. "No, you're fine back there," I said. He'd be on his feet carrying bags all day, so he might as well stretch out.

"If I clock in early, they don't pay me until the hour starts. But they'll tell me to get busy just the same."

"Don't work for free, Claude. If they got money to build this place, they got money to pay you. I'm on the clock, so you might as well keep me company until the plane gets here."

Claude switched hats, folded the corduroy into his satchel, and put in its place the red porter's cap.

"Glad you stopped."

"It's what I do. Seems strange to leave somebody walking with an empty backseat."

"Some won't bother, though. Especially chauffeurs. They'll pass in a hurry and kick dirt up in your face in a hot minute. Scared their white folks might find out they rode somebody."

"The man I work for won't give me any grief for riding you and Yvette. If he still lived here he'd be walking, too."

Claude gave me a look, and then he turned his eyes all around the car, from the ceiling's stitching down to the pinstripe upholstery and the heartwood floorboards. He stared at everything like my boss's name was stitched somewhere, an autograph in silver thread. They do good work in Detroit, but mine wasn't factory. The custom work gave that old car a second life, new guts on good bone. It might as well look better than it did the first time around.

"He lives in Los Angeles now, but he was born here. Stopped over in Chicago to see some family on his way, but he's on the next flight. I want you to get his bags for me."

"What's his name? I like to know their names when they get off the plane."

"You'll know his name when you see him. Nat Cole's on that flight."

"Nat King Cole?"

"Yep. Nat King Cole."

"Coming here? To Montgomery?"

"This is home. If a man can't come home, then home ain't about much."

I looked through the rearview, but Claude wasn't looking at me. Seemed he was staring at the radio that was quiet just then. Whatever he heard he was spinning in his head.

"How old are you?" I asked him.

"Twenty-one. Well, I will be come January."

"You remember what happened last time Nat Cole was here?"

"From people talk about it. Gang of white boys came out of nowhere. They say one jumped all over him. Then the white boy got jumped on. Some soldier."

"They tell you what happened after?"

"Sent the soldier off to Kilby. Hell, he might still be there."

"No, I'm out now, Claude. Been free for a year and some change. Went to California, but I'm home for a spell."

He touched the bill of that cap and tipped it just so, and then he pulled it off completely.

"Welcome home."

We do that hat tip for all kinds of reasons. Respecting somebody's home. Speaking of the dead and buried. Excuse me and much obliged and farewell and anything else.

"You know anybody in Kilby, Claude?"

He said so and called a name; the whole while his fingers and nerves made a handful of taps on that hat, the patent leather hard as a tambourine.

"You pray for him then. Write him a letter and tell him you're praying for him. Then pray for him some more. Even if he gets out. You pray they don't send him back."

The hat went back on his head, and he nodded while he straightened it.

"Why you come back from California? I damn sure wouldn't come back."

"A few good reasons. People need to see my face to know I'm still here."

If I said more I would have to say it all. And it was ten until the hour by then, and we both had schedules to keep.

"The young lady. You asked her on a date yet?"

The stammering told me the answer even if he couldn't outright.

"Sounds like you want to see her somewhere else besides this road every day."

"Yeah, but I want to make it nice. Not just a movie or something. Some place real nice. You know what I mean?"

"I know exactly."

I pulled a twenty from my billfold, young, fresh-cut money that had not seen many hands other than mine.

"That's yours for this business I need you to take care of. Nat's getting off that plane with his road manager. Skip will handle his own bag. Nat's got two. I don't like to carry his bags, because I need to watch for trouble. Need to have my hands free."

He looked at my fingers then, that bit of mangle and the knuckle swelling that never went away, some from the war and some from Kilby.

"That won't be a problem," he said, and folded that money in his pocket.

"Second thing, I want you to talk to Yvette this afternoon. Ask her to the Centennial Ballroom tonight. You asked why I came back. To give you a show."

Claude Washington, Carver ballplayer who could run a country mile, needed a second to catch his breath.

"I believe I can. Absolutely," he told me. He smoothed that chest pocket like the money needed tending. "I thank you. My eagle came a little early this week."

"How it's supposed to be. Make your own paydays, Claude."

He breathed out one good time. That all-county-everything voice came back.

"Only thing is, Nat Cole doing a show in town and I haven't heard a thing about it. I'm kind of nosy, and something like that I'd know about."

"Kind of a secret, for a few more hours at least. Last time the whole world knew Nat Cole was on his way, and the wrong folks were ready for some trouble. They need to stay in the dark. But since you like to hear things on the vine, now you can be the one to spread the word."

"Seems like he'd be downtown somewhere. The Paramount or the Empire or some such."

"You couldn't sit in the front row downtown, now could you? When I say this show is for you and yours, I mean it."

"What about the white folks?"

"Not your worry."

A chauffeur parked right behind me and got out to clean the grille of his people's Cadillac. It was easier while the metal was still hot, but the grime looked like pine tar with needles and sawdust mixed in. That driver was wiping so hard, he was liable to break a sweat. Maybe he worked for some of that old money up in lumber country. He had his work cut out, trying to keep the shine without scratching the chrome.

"Me and Yvette in the front row."

Not the least bit of question in what Claude said. He just liked the way it sounded, as he should have. On that night when Nat Cole was attacked, I had been in the balcony with a girl and all kinds of plans in my head. Those forever kind of plans.

"White tablecloth. Candle. A little card on the table with your name on it. Just like we do it in Los Angeles, on Central Avenue and Sunset and whatnot."

He looked off somewhere, his mind already sent on ahead to the evening.

"What if she says no?"

"She walks through that dust with you every morning, so it seems like she'd be keen on a show."

His soles tapped against the pine of the floorboards. Maybe Claude was a pacer, walking back and forth when he had something on his mind. The tapping turned to the scrape of him pivoting, to look through the back window toward the runway in the middle of that pastureland. There it was, not much to see yet, but the plane had dipped under the lowest of the clouds.

"Here he comes now, on his way to give you a show, my friend," I said.

Claude opened his door in a hurry, and I heard an engine. It wasn't the plane's noise, because the propellers were too far to hear that turning. On the other side of the near fence, another redcap sat on a tractor hooked to a flatbed meant for the luggage.

"What's Mr. Cole carrying?"

"Two Hartmann cases."

"The rawhide ones or waxed?"

"Waxed."

"Good. Rawhide looks old after a while. The waxed hold up nice. They ought to look like the money you pay, if you ask me."

One last question before he closed the door.

"That one who jumped on Nat Cole. Some people say you beat that cracker with a trombone. I heard some say trumpet. I'm wondering which way is true."

"Neither. I beat him with a microphone."

Claude tipped that hat once more, and I noticed then the rough patch in the patent leather where his fingers had rubbed away the gloss.

"See you inside, Mr. Weary."

By the time Claude had walked around to the side door, the plane had turned to a spark, the sun flashing on the metal as bright as it burned when it came out the furnace. Eastern flights used to land just down the road from Kilby at the old Gunter Air Base. The guards would march hoe squads down there to clear the kudzu off the fences around the runways. Air traffic towers looked just like the

ones at the prison. The guards who manned those walk-
ways looked down on us ready for somebody to run. The
men who did always died. The only question was whether
it was the twelve-gauge or a carbine that put him down.

I hated the sight of an airplane, and the sound of them
and their night flying was even worse. First it was army
air corps and the air force after, with jets moving faster
than sound. Sleeping on a Kilby tier was hard enough,
but the noise and rumble, hearing free-world folks come
and go as they pleased, was just one more thing to rack
my mind.

So when I stepped out of the car and saw that clean shot
line between me and the control tower, I had to stay in
my right-now mind, let my fingers be my watch and com-
pass, tell me where I was and when. I came on back to the
moment before me, in time to see the plane, lower then,
close enough to read the letters, and big enough to throw
a wide shadow over the wire grass.

The Christmas carols on the terminal's speakers
sounded like they were coming through a can. They had
been stripped of anything colorful or sharp. The static
popped louder than the drumbeat, and the only thing that
made it sound like anything was the fact that the music
was old and familiar. Los Angeles had spoiled me. I had
experienced the pleasure of sitting in the Capitol Records

studios, listening to songs fresh-made. Most music fell short after that.

The row of airport televisions cost a nickel for fifteen minutes, enough time to watch Nat's television show from beginning to end. Of course, the show was a month gone, and it wasn't coming back. The sales department at NBC said nobody was willing to pay, but if every television had a coin box like the ones in the Dannelly Field lobby, then they'd find plenty of folks willing to ante up.

Midway down the terminal, the colored waiting sign had bright lights behind the letters, a Negro marquee. A few of the drivers sat in there and got a bit of break-fast at the sandwich window on the back end of the lunch counter. In the waiting area, children stood at the picture windows, and some sat on grown folks' shoulders, waiting to see the plane land. They pressed their fingers onto the glass. A cleaning lady, her name tag too far to read, paid no mind to the landing. She stood near the window with a spray can of Windex and a rag, ready to clean the smudges as soon as the people were gone.

Outside, Claude stood beside the other porters, milling with their backs to the windows. The man on the tractor had unhooked the flatbed and traded it out for the narrow stairs he would haul to the plane. No sooner than that plane stopped moving, wheels first and then the propellers, those men had the bags off. Nat's never touched that wagon, because Claude was on point, earning every dollar and then some.

Skip was first out of the shadow of the plane's door, and then came Nat Cole, his feet on Alabama ground.

"Here we are, friend."

That's what Nat told me when he came through the door. It was something he said when we pulled into his regular places. NBC. Capitol Records. *Here we are, friend.* Good days and the lesser days. Like getting there was part of the show, too.

I walked catty-corner to Nat, a step or two behind and just off to the right. Back in his prizefighting days, Skip was a southpaw, and he carried his bag in his right hand as he walked beside me. Once Claude fell in behind, the four of us passed through Dannelly Field like a shotgun house wind, a straight line from the back door to the front.

When we made it to the sidewalk, that Montgomery City Lines bus pulled in right beside us. That airport bus was not the one that had made the place famous. The notorious one rolled up Cleveland Avenue and made its way to the Court Square Fountain, but they all were kindred. If it wasn't Mrs. Parks's bus, it was the one young Miss Colvin had been thrown off months before. Those were the women I knew about. I couldn't think of them without wondering about the unknown folks who got manhandled and laughed at, never speaking a word about it after.

The three bus riders were white folks, and once they were off, the bus carried only its driver with that pistol on his hip, nickel-plated with a chestnut handle. I neither stopped walking nor flinched. I had learned to hide any worry or tremble deep down in my gut, leave it where I had buried so much already.

Seeing that empty bus, I hoped that every Monday evening, when they used to watch Nat's show, they would have walked a little faster to get home, let that television be something to wrap the evening around. With the show dead, I had to bring him in person, give the folks the show I had aimed to see those years before.

The show must go on was something singers were supposed to say, but I'd seen plenty of singers and never once had I heard one say it. I knew they lived it though. Skip told me about the time Nat finished a New York show and left the stage with a stomach full of blood. Leaving it half-done was unthinkable to the man. He only had two shows he didn't finish properly, and both ate at him as bad as that ulcer did. One was on television, and there was nothing I could do to change that. But the other was the concert I'd witnessed, the mob rushing him and the band onstage. That one, live from Montgomery, we'd try one more time.

Skip got in the passenger's side, and I let Nat in the back. I walked around to the trunk while Claude loaded the bags.

"You just don't know what's bound to happen when you get up in the morning, do you, Mr. Weary?" Claude told me.

"Damn sure don't. That's why I don't save my good liquor. Neither should you. Top-shelf all evening."

Nat put his right hand out the window and gave Claude a shake, a good word, and another bill to add to his pocket. Then we were off, driving our quiet miles into Montgomery proper. I'd set up my Packard just like the Cadillac in Nat's driveway, the car we made our way around Los Angeles in. I had filled the wicker box with staff paper, a handful of sharp pencils, and a couple packs of Kools. He liked to write while he rode. Maybe his hometown would spark something better than the memory.

The last time Nat Cole was in Alabama, a mob tried to kill him. I stopped them, and paid for it with ten good years. I had brought him home, and I would make sure the show happened this time, from the first bit of hand-clapping when he took the stage to the last bit when the show ended. I would watch from my seat at the side of the stage, hidden in a nice bit of shadow where I could see everything.

I had planned to give something to the folks in Montgomery, but there was some selfishness in it, too. The evening was meant for me as much as anybody else. I needed new songs in my head, because I had spent my empty years living in what could have been. That old, lonesome show that haunted me had been playing for much too long.

Chapter 2

Mattie kept straightening things that weren't even crooked. Her hat. Her collar. No need for it, though, because she looked as beautiful as ever, as if not a day had passed during the war, as if we hadn't fought a war at all. Maybe beauty was a private little miracle given to those who had been forced to love across the ocean. Time had been set backward, so that when we all got home, the world was waiting in the same place we had left it.

"I hope he doesn't mind a picture," Mattie said. "He must get tired of people asking him all the time."

"I'm sure he's used to it by now. He won't mind at all."

She ran a finger around the camera's lens, and flicked the dust from her glove. Of course there was no dust to speak of, because she had been running her fingers across that lens the whole time we sat in the back of my brother's taxi, riding across town to the Empire Theater.

Her camera was a simple, elegant thing, a red leather box that looked something like a gift.

She had taken a picture of the marquee as we made the turn from Dexter Avenue. NAT COLE TRIO. He was the most famous man, black or white, ever to be born in my hometown, but that sign was a first for us back then. A Negro name with that much light behind it. In Montgomery that was rare.

"You're sure he won't mind?"

Mattie smoothed her collar again and breathed her nerves away.

"Absolutely. He won't mind one bit," I told her.

Nat Cole was a friend of mine. He was born in Montgomery a few months before me. When Miss McCarthy called the roll on the first day of kindergarten, I answered when I heard my name.

"Nathaniel—"

"Present."

"Not yet, Master Weary."

As it turned out, two Nathaniels sat in that classroom at Montgomery County Training School. The first on the roll was Nathaniel Adams Cole. It seemed we were both a little surprised that our names weren't ours alone. At the same time, I was glad to know I had at least one thing in common with somebody. By third grade, I was the only Nathaniel left. Like many of the families in Bel-Air, Nat and his people had gone to Chicago.

He went up there and got himself famous. "Montgomery's Very Own Nat Cole Battles the Legendary Earl Hines in Chicago." The papers added "Montgomery's Very Own" like it was his given name. For a while Eddie Cole's name was bigger than his younger brother's. "Sepia Records Presents Montgomery's Very Own Eddie Cole and His Solid Swingers." And months later the stories read "The Cole Brothers and Their Solid Swingers." Finally, the name was Nat's alone.

Before the war I worked with my family, driving a taxi from our stand on Jackson Street. Nat Cole was good cab conversation whenever his songs came on the radio. *You know, he was born right here.* He played the kind of music that made people feel generous enough to kick in an extra penny or two in tip money, as though Nat's crooning could get somebody from here to there a little bit faster, make the ride that much smoother.

Nat was good barbershop conversation next door to the cabstand at Malden Brothers.

You know, he's from right here.

Samuel Malden would say it every time a song came on, sometimes pointing his razor to the floor, as though Nat had sprung up through the clay and the earth, straight through the concrete and the black-and-white floor.

Martha Gray said it, too. *You know, he's from right here,* when anyone brought his records to the counter of her shop around the corner on High Street. Though the top-forty slots reserved for the hit makers changed every Tuesday, Nat always had a place reserved. Nat Cole never really left, though he had been gone from Montgomery for all those years.

George Worthy said it, too, on his radio show, *Hometown Serenade*. *You know, friends, he's from right here.* George put a little bit more space between the words and talked in a whisper, his voice turned down and softened, a little brush on a snare drum. *Right here.* The station's signal came through strong on Centennial Hill. They played Nat's songs that evening, but in the back of that cab on the way to the show, his voice got weaker as we crossed from the Hill to downtown. Soon after, the voice was gone altogether.

The theater district was foreign to us and governed by different rules, going through side doors and sitting in balconies. Every so often, though, the closed doors were minded by a Negro janitor or doorman who I knew from the neighborhood. Mr. Cartwright had cleaned up at the Empire for as long as I'd known him, and he was just then sitting by the back door. The coin I pressed into his hand was newly minted, a half-dollar with Booker T. Washing-

ton's face looking sideways from Mr. Cartwright's fingertips.

"Son, you don't have to do that."

"I want to, Mr. Cartwright. Besides, it ain't about have
to."

He held the money for a while, flipped it over a couple of
times, head and tail of Booker T. spinning.

"Appreciate you," he said, and the door opened to us as
long as no one found out.

I wanted to take a picture with Nat before the show and
also have a word. I had a ring in my pocket. I had been
waiting for that night to give it to Mattie, and who better
for a serenade than Nat King Cole, born across town and a
friend for all those years.

I heard the trio of voices on the other side of the dressing room door. In the mix of them, one was unmistakably
Nat. Mattie turned her head and brought her ear a little
bit closer to the door. She held her camera as if every picture she'd ever taken was still inside. Surely, the picture
we would take with Nat would end up in a frame somewhere in the little house for sale on Tuscaloosa Street that
I'd seen that morning. It'd be perfect for us. I had peeked
through the gap in the blue-striped curtains. Maybe the
picture would sit above the mantel, along with pictures of
the wedding, the children, and all the rest to come.

After the show, we would go back across town to the Centennial Hotel and do some drinking in the Majestic Lounge. We would go up on the rooftop garden and stand in the middle of the cabbage palms in the night light. I had told Mattie, right there, years before, what she surely knew already, that I loved her. I'd tell her again with a ring, and once she said yes, we would go back down to the Majestic, where Nat, Oscar, and Johnny would surely play like the bands always did after their downtown shows.

I had a newfound taste for big-money liquor, and I had my GI money and a bankroll fat enough to buy one for everybody in the narrow little bar. I'd order some of that top-shelf bourbon that had gotten dusty, waiting for somebody to have a night worth reaching up that high to bring the bottle down for.

But before all of that I would have to ask Nat. Before I could ask him, I had to knock.

Mattie beat me to it, though. She knocked, glove against the steel, and the hollow door echoed loud enough to fill the empty hallway. Mattie smiled and nodded once more, calm then, as if the last of her nerves had flowed through her knuckles and bounced back and forth between the metal sides of the door.

We waited, listening for the footsteps of someone coming to let us in. I turned the knob, unlocked, and pushed the door to find a dark, empty room. Nothing moved but me, and I could see myself more shadow than reflection in the many mirrors, each framed in darkened bulbs that carried no light of their own, only the little bit that came from the hallway.

The voices we had heard were a little louder inside, and I saw why that was. The ducts overhead carried the sound, and we had been fooled by the echoes. The voices came from an unmarked door we had passed walking in.

When I pushed it open, I didn't see anybody at first. It was a storage room stacked with marquee letters as tall as we were. They were the same set used to spell the names of the trio of men—Nat, Oscar, Johnny—sitting in the corner on worn-out theater seats.

"Is that who I think it is?" Nat said when he saw me, his seat snapping closed behind him when he rose to his feet.

"Guess that depends on who's thinking," I said. "And who's being thought of."

"Good old Nat Weary."

"Ol' Nat Cole."

When the boys saw Mattie, they all stood.

"Mattie. It's been a long time, but the years have been more than kind," Nat told her.

"And you as well."

"It feels like a long time ago, but I guess everything before the war does now."

It felt good to be remembered. They had come to

Montgomery in the fall of 1941, playing for the college's Autumn Ball. Mattie had wondered if he would remember. Four years was not a long time, but Nat was right about the wartime years. They made even the best memories seem that much further away.

The marks of their work covered their palms. Oscar's and Johnny's fingers were more calloused than mine had become after years of holding a rifle like it was my last friend in the world. Oscar had those long nails like the guitar players who worked every Saturday night on the Hill and down Jackson Street, and the shoulder of his jacket had creases from the leather strap. Johnny had the same marks in a different place, rubs along his lapel where the bass rested. Their suits were work clothes a shade lighter than my army green, but made from shiny thread that caught the same light the pomade on their heads did.

"Would it be too much to ask you gentlemen for a photograph?" Mattie lifted that camera when she asked them. The way she said "gentlemen," with that lilt in her voice, made the word sound like the flick of her fingernail on crystal.

They were more than willing, but the light wasn't doing us any favors. Three fixtures dangled from the ceiling, barely fixtures at all, just sockets on the end of dusty cloth wires. We arranged ourselves, the five of us, in that little bit of dingy light. We would be halfway in the shadows no matter where we stood in that storeroom, as far away from starlight as we could ever be.

"This won't do," she told them, her chin up and her eyes on the slim little fixtures. "All that light across the hall going to waste."

"I do say, ma'am. I believe you have a point," Oscar said. Then he motioned to me. I was, after all, the one closest to the door. Mattie shrugged and lifted the camera again.

"They won't miss that little bit of light we borrow," she said.

And with a look to see that no one was coming, we made our march a few steps across the hall to the dressing room that on most nights was home to the star of the show. I felt along the wall until I found the switch. When all that light pushed through the dressing room mirrors, we went with it. We didn't have to share that space with anyone other than our smiling reflections.

"Perfect." Mattie placed us just so and then she stood in the middle, facing the mirror and holding the camera before her. She clicked three shots.

"There. Just like that," she said.

Before I left for the army, Mattie had asked an odd promise of me. She didn't want letters. Just pictures. Her uncle had died in the First World War, and her grand-mother held on to his letters, going over his words so many times that the paper got too old and raggedy to read. The pictures were different. Her grandmother would never see his grave, Mattie told me, but she could see his face as he stood on a bridge near Lorraine, the last of the distant places he would see in his twenty-three years of living.

I kept that promise. All she knew of my time came through the little portraits of faraway countrysides spared from the bombing. She sent to me as much of home as she could get that lens on. I had missed her voice, which just then, with that camera in her hands, made the simplest requests: "Sweetheart, raise your chin for me. Oscar, turn this way a little bit, please. Thank you."

"Just a few more," she said.

"Take your time," Nat told her.

I was tempted to ask her right then. I wondered how the engagement ring would look with all of that dressing room starlight passing through it.

"I got a ring," I told Nat.

I said this just loud enough for only him to hear, once Mattie had moved back for a few wider pictures. Nat patted me on the shoulder as Mattie told us to look her way.

"We're headed to the Majestic after the show," I said. "I was hoping you could sing something for us when you get back across town."

"You waited long enough, my friend," he said. "How about we start the show with the two of you? Sing your song first in front of all of Montgomery. Be the envy of this little town."

"Even better."

"I'll stop the show. Then you'll know what to do next."

I nodded and felt his words in my chest, where they sank in deep. Nat had transformed my little plan, stoking the fires of a wondrous notion.

I was there on Saint John Street when Nat Cole got his new middle name. Adams was out and in its place, King. We grew up in the little Bel-Air houses, all with green trim and white clapboard siding like they'd grown from the same handful of seed. Nat Cole lived on the end of the block, next to the lot we turned into our playground. Sometimes he played with us and sometimes he stayed home practicing on that front-room piano with the door and windows open.

In the middle of "I'll Fly Away" and "Just a Closer Walk with Thee," Nat would work in a riff from the school yard hymns. The rope jumping and the marble shooting and the whatnot would stop, and he'd know it was on account of our listening and every so often singing along. The one that everybody knew was "Old King Cole was a merry old soul and a merry old soul was he."

He had a famous man's name before he was either

famous or a man. I could lie and say I knew where he was headed, but it would only be a half lie. His hands were suited for a star turn, but I figured it would come from that work he did on that makeshift diamond we called a ball field. We had no hind-catcher, just a tree stump with cans on top. Instead of hearing "Wade in the Water" and "I'm on My Way to Canaan Land," anybody who saw Nat Cole on the mound heard the sound of that curveball catching the corner of a tin can. The sound of his strikes rang out like his music did.

At seven years old, Nat Cole threw curveballs with either hand. His left coming at you like Big Walker, and that right like Satchel Paige. And when it wasn't baseball it was marbles, where Nat Cole could put enough English on a cat's-eye to send us all home empty-handed and head scratching. We should have known from the sound of the strikes and the clink of marbles in keepsies. It didn't occur to us that all of his winning ways, a left hand as good as the right, came from that same piano playing he did when he sent "Old King Cole" out of his window, floating down the street and carrying that nickname. Maybe it was a stretch to say we gave it to him, when he gave it to us first.

After Mattie and I exited through the side door, we took our place in the second of the two lines on the Montgomery Street sidewalk. The first line started near the marquee, and the white patrons were damn near close enough to touch the letters, stretched over the walkway as big as war headlines. The value of the marquee, outside of telling who's playing and when, was that it gave a little shelter if it rained.

It could have been raining on us in the other line, which led to the little box office with that sign in the window, COLORED SEATING, that let us know we were in the right place. Above our heads was nothing but three stories of brick wall, the fire escape, and the sky. We waited beyond a rope that, exposed to the weather, had not been velvet in years.

The black cabbies knew which end of the block to leave their fares, and three of our orange cars were among them. My mother and father both drove their Hudsons, and my brother, Dane, drove the Studebaker. At that time of night, he could make it from the Empire to Centennial Hill in six minutes. Another minute and a half would get him from the Court Square Fountain to the capitol steps and that statue of Jefferson Davis. A few more turns got him over to Union and south on High Street all the way across town to Jackson and the cabstand. There the city became ours again, where the State Theater marquee did for us what the one above the Empire could not, keep the rain off our heads while we waited for a show.

I had been raised to believe that if I timed it just right in my taxi, I could outrun Jim Crow. He was not fast or skillful, because he did not have to be. He could always corner us somewhere and make us wait. If I moved quickly and kept to schedule, I could leave him somewhere looking at my taillights. When I drove that cab, the elusiveness was possible. But standing still in the other line, Jim Crow had me where he wanted me. Nat's plan was enough to elevate me for a while, but then I felt Jim Crow's ass while he sat upon my shoulder, sweating out the starch of my army uniform, leaving creases where they didn't belong.

We stood beneath the heroes in the wall posters, matinee specials of soldiers old and new. John Wayne and Anthony Quinn, and, for good measure, they had brought back old Howard Hughes and his *Hell's Angels*. Hollywood had sent its armies to sit sentry, keeping watch over Saturday night. Those of us below them—sailors, nurses, a pilot or two—wore the wartime colors that we'd saved Europe in. We had gotten as far as the Empire and its velvet rope, where we waited for somebody to open the door.

When Nat Cole played the 1941 Autumn Ball, he had filled the Centennial Ballroom. We hadn't seen that kind of commotion since Erskine Hawkins came back from Harlem. Nat was not altogether famous, but famous enough. That

was the first time I had heard him play since we were children. One hand was Chicago fast, and the other nice and
slow, like some country boy straight out the woods and in
no hurry to go back home.

During a break, Mattie and I eased up close to the
piano, where I had thought that I might say hello to "my
old friend Nat" to impress my date. I thought better of it,
because so much time had passed. People changed, as
they should. If I had left Montgomery for Chicago, then
left Chicago for Los Angeles, my birthplace might feel
small and distant. I didn't expect him to recognize me, but
I was sure glad he did.

"Good ol' Nat Weary!"

"Good ol' Nat Cole," I said. Mattie looked at me like I
was on a whole different shelf right then.

You could still hear a little bit of Alabama in his voice,
secondhand by way of Chicago and California, but it was
there just the same.

When I introduced him to Mattie, he greeted her with
a smile and nod. They talked about "Honeysuckle Rose,"
and she told him she liked what he did with "Song of the
Wanderer," different than what Erskine Hawkins and
Count Basie had done. She spoke as calm as could be, the
whole time her hands dug into my arm, strong enough to
pull the elbow clean off. Once Nat started the second set,
I felt the lighter touch of her fingers, practiced on pianos

since she was a child. She played notes down my arm, "Dream a Little Dream of Me" and a little of the song that came after, a medley that ended with her fingers in mine.

Mattie whispered the names of the songs I didn't know, and as the evening went on, she whispered all manner of preludes to the night that was our beginning. We'd met in a lecture hall, and what had started as talk across desk rows had taken on a new form. It had turned into a long-felt touch in those weeks that led autumn into winter, as we enjoyed the wonders of articulated love.

Then came Pearl Harbor. As a part-time student and part-time cab driver, my number had come up among the first. Mattie and I were left with the bits of each other that could fit in the white frame of photographs we sent across the ocean. Every so often, a wartime radio was close enough for us to hear a Nat Cole record and that faint sound of home. Victory brought me back. On either end of my war years were those two shows of Nat Cole's. That old one at the Centennial and the one I waited for with Mattie's hand on my arm and her ring in my pocket.

Nine of them would play the show. Nat at the piano. Oscar on guitar. Johnny on bass. The rest were horns, six of them, their positions set on the bandstand at the back of the stage. They were local players who marched with the

Bama State band. The New Collegians, they called themselves. The piano was separated from the bandstand by a screen decorated with autumn leaves in red, white, and blue, matching the bunting that lined the stage. During the shows I'd seen at the Empire, the thin fabric of the screen revealed only the shadows and lines of the bandstand. Once the music started, the screen would show them as it rose, lifting the music and applause right along with it.

From the first row of the colored balcony we could see most everything. Too small a consolation. After Mattie set her camera on the floor, she nudged me. The seats in the front row downstairs were filling, including the two that we'd sat in after we left the dressing room. Perhaps the starlight had emboldened us, and with no ushers around and the outside doors still closed, we made ourselves comfortable in the forbidden row, if only for a few seconds, before we eased back outside. A young couple took the same seats, with the man unfolding my A4 for his lady friend and then taking A3, where Mattie had been. I'm sure he found his cushion sunk a little bit lower because of the beautiful crater left by Miss Mattie Green, more lovely and buxom than Jean Harlow, Betty Grable, or the young lady who held his arm. Mattie had run her hand along my collar and my ear, and then down the back of the downstairs seat, collecting army green and red velvet lint on her gloves. She'd rolled it between her fingers and released a bright little tornado that spun to the floor.

Our actual seats were worn, but sturdy enough. Besides, once the music stopped, everyone in that theater would want to be in my place, AA17. That ring had been with me for the seven hours since I'd bought it, but I had lived with the notion for years. People had rushed to altars all over Montgomery before the war, but I didn't want to. *In case I might die* wasn't the way I wanted to start things. I needed it to feel like forever instead of maybe.

"I wonder what song he'll play first?" Mattie said. "I guess it doesn't matter, because I want to hear them all."

I just squeezed her arm. I didn't want to say much until I said the most important thing. The nerves had started working, and I needed the last few minutes to get collected. No fumbling with the pocket button or dropping the ring.

On my way out, I'd told Mr. Cartwright about the plan me and Nat had made, and then I'd given him three more half-dollar coins, one more for him and two for the stage-hands above our heads, moving on the catwalk that ran down the center of the theater, their own little alley high above us. One turned right and the other left as they took their places on the twin spotlights that flanked the stage. One looked across and nodded my way.

The blinking of the house lights came and went, and the place got showtime dark. The New Collegians came on, and the applause started, polite from downstairs and heavier in the balcony, where some of the folks probably knew the band members. As the horn players took their seats on the bandstand, Johnny, Oscar, and Nat came on to roars and clapping from the top and bottom of the theater. As soon as Nat took his place at the piano, the band started with a little of the local flavor with "Tuxedo Junction." Then Nat leaned into the microphone and told us what we already knew.

"Good evening, Montgomery. We are the Nat Cole Trio and we're pleased to be here tonight with the wonderful New Collegians ensemble. It's good to be back home."

Hearing him say "home" brought more cheers. When he lifted his hands from the piano, the band stopped as well. One of the two spotlights left the stage and swung around to me.

"Montgomery," he sang. "Let me tell you 'bout a friend of mine . . ."

And then it was my turn.

Mattie watched me drop to a knee. My back foot stepped onto the folks beside us, but they seemed to understand. I took Mattie by both hands, and everything about her said yes. People downstairs were on their feet. A few from the rows beneath the balcony had walked into the aisle to see. Sweet murmurs came from the seats all around us. I was never one who liked being the center of things, never craved the attention of anyone beyond my loved ones and friends, but that feeling was something else, the whole world knowing the good news I'd held in my pocket for too long.

I froze before I could reach for the ring. My heart beat faster than it had since the war. It was not because of love, marriage, or the fear of either. Through the brass railings along the balcony, I saw the trouble coming. The usher moved down the far-side aisle, walking faster than any usher needed to. He was already five rows from the stage. He didn't search out seats, and he had no patrons behind him. He looked at Nat, who didn't see him because he was looking at me like everyone else in the Empire.

"Nathaniel," Mattie said, more a question than my name.

By then she was looking over the rail, seeing what I did down below, just as that usher jumped the stage. His flashlight hit the floorboards as he pushed himself up. The spotlight showed that it wasn't a flashlight at all. It was a foot and a half of lead pipe.

Nat and the band played softly, "Somebody Loves Me,"

but it was loud enough to mask the footsteps of the man crossing the stage.

Mattie saw it, too. "Somebody—"

That's when I shouted and jumped over the railing. I was again at the foot of the stage, pain running up both legs from the jolt of that fall. I stumbled up the stairs, trying to get to the piano before the man with the pipe did. But I didn't. Nat by then had turned and stood, moving just enough so that the pipe meant for his head hit his shoulder instead. The thud, more flesh than bone, sent both men to the ground.

The band shouted in the middle of the ruckus going on behind the screen. The attack stopped the show before the screen lifted, and a half-dozen men, some with pipes and some throwing punches, had rushed the bandstand from the back. Nat was alone in front of the piano, grabbing at the man's shirt, the cotton so thin that it ripped, freeing the attacker to rear back with the pipe again.

I got in front of him before he could hit Nat, but he was quick enough to catch me in the side of the knee. Not a good shot, but good enough for me to stumble. Before he could square up, I grabbed the microphone that had fallen to the floor against my foot. I swung, and the first blow sent him back against the piano. I kept swinging, and the sound of the steel against his skull went through the Empire, and the screaming from the place got quiet. I swung some more, beating him until the microphone broke to pieces and went dead.

The police had poured in, and two of them pulled me off him. I stood in the middle of the stage with cops on each arm. By then, the attacker was on his feet, squared up with me. I had broken his nose, and his right eye was already swelling. In spite of all that, he smiled and puckered his lips to spit a long bloody shot that caught my ear. The rest hit one of the police. And as the officer raised his hand to his face, he let go of my right arm, so I swung again. I leaned into that punch enough to free the last of his teeth and send him off the stage headfirst.

As the police led me to the side door, the applause started, because Nat was walking to the front of the stage. Though he favored his right side, he was upright. He looked toward me, not a nod or a smile, but just a look that said as much. He took a long breath, or at least tried to. An army corporal set the piano bench right and moved it toward Nat, but he said thank you and no. Seemed he had something to say, and everybody got quiet to hear. But he didn't talk. He waved his good arm and began to sing. "Got the world on a string . . ."

Behind the screen, the band picked up the instruments and started playing. As raggedy as the whole affair had been through the free-for-all, the music was clean again and moving straight ahead. The New Collegians were outnumbered by the audience, drowned by the murmuring of folks still stunned. Once the band started playing, it was like a new kind of wind rolled in and the ruckus that had clouded the place cleared out. Nat had no microphone so his hands carried the song instead.

I looked for Mattie in the balcony, but the upstairs audience had crowded the railings. And the police moved me out the door and toward one of the squad cars parked every which way in the alley. People in the Whitfield Hotel had the windows wide open, looking down. I thought maybe the police wouldn't beat me just yet. They'd at least wait until we got to the station. My stomach got tight, my jaw, too, waiting for the first of them to swing. But then they left me in the car and went back to the door. I heard the piano, too. And I was thankful that his fingers had not been smashed.

Mr. Cartwright ran up to the side of the car. "That cracker would have sure enough killed him, son. You did right."

He looked back at the door, but the police had their backs to us. They were listening. "I've Got the World on a String" sounded so sweet. In spite of everything, that was the honest truth. I won't lie and say the music made me forget that I was in a car, handcuffs and all. The band made the most of it, doing what they could.

"I wish I could have helped you, son. In my heart, I was up there swinging."

"You can help me now."

"I'm too old to bust anybody out."

"No, sir. The ring in my shirt pocket," I told him. "You need to take it and the money."

"You want me to give it to your lady friend?" he asked.

"No, sir. Not like this. To my people at the cabstand. If it's in my pocket when they take my clothes at the jail, that'll be the last I see of it."

He reached in and took hold of the ring.

"She down there looking for you," he said, motioning down the block to Montgomery Street, where Mattie was looking into the backs of police cars. Mr. Cartwright waved to her, and she came running.

"Are you hurt?" she said, breathless.

"No. I just wanted to make sure you made it out all right."

"Me? I didn't know if they were out here— Lord, I just didn't want you to be someplace with nobody knowing where."

"Don't worry."

"Where in the hell did they come from?"

"Crawled out the gutter somewhere."

Her hands shook, and the gloves showed it that much more.

"They'll make me spend the night in jail," I told her. "I'll pay my fine and be out before noon Monday. I'll meet you for lunch."

"It's not funny."

"It will be once it's over," I said.

The music had stopped by then. I could barely see the cops for all the people that had crowded in behind them to get a glimpse of Nat Cole finishing the only song he would play that evening.

I need to see a doctor, and I'm afraid I cannot continue. Good night, Montgomery.

And the applause then was as loud as the hollering, begging him to stay, but they knew he could not. Nat King Cole had been attacked in the city where he was born. He had left once before, and he was forced to leave again. If he never returned nobody could blame him. I damn sure couldn't.

"Tell my people," I told Mattie. "I'm sorry. I just wanted us to have a night."

I just wanted it to be done with. Take me to jail, let the judge talk to me any kind of way on Monday as long as I could pay my fine and do thirty days.

"It'll be fine, sweetheart. I'll see you soon." That was all I could say to her.

Mr. Cartwright walked Mattie away before the cops returned. When my brother's cab came to the end of the block, he hollered for Mattie to come and get in. They waited so that they could follow us and make sure I was taken to the jail and not back in the woods somewhere. Dane followed as close as he could, but he couldn't make the red light the officers sped through, with those sirens so loud they never left my ears. We made it to the jailhouse faster than I could have imagined.

Chapter 3

I saw the judge that Tuesday after Armistice Day. Getting locked up on a holiday weekend meant an extra night in jail. The courthouse was closed that Monday, but the parades had come close enough for us to hear the marching bands. That music was worse than the waiting and the silence in the jailhouse, waiting to see what they gave me. Wondering. Praying.

Every man in that corridor that Tuesday morning was quiet, because the deputies watching us demanded as much. We waited our turns, lined up along the windows. It was the first decent light I had seen in three days, so I stole a face full of whatever I could see. Down on the courthouse steps, a growing line of soldiers stood with their wives-to-be. More of them gathered on the narrow lawn, all ready for their turns before some other judge. It had become regular business downtown, the courthouse weddings. A marriage license was free for a man in uniform.

Because so many came, a clerk would draw names from a hat, and a little bit of whooping would come after she read each one. They all brought flowers, and petals covered the courthouse grass the same as the leaves did. Newlyweds left in cars with ration cans tied to the bumpers, and that tapping on Ripley Street cobblestones carried farther than the voices.

Bunting covered every bit of courtroom wood and railing, upstairs and down. The judge had his picture on the wall, and his chest was poked out and swollen. Every lawyer in the courthouse had come home with a medal on him, it seemed. The colors that lined every street between Paris and home were meant to make us all feel victorious. I had carried that bit of pride, too, before they dressed me in jailhouse colors. They had taken my uniform from me before they snapped my picture, turned me sideways and snapped again. They lied to the world and acted like I had never fought, but Lord knows I had. And in those moments when I did my cold and heavy remembering, I was again in that place.

I had made it up Utah Beach with the Battery D boys of the 333rd. After Brittany I spent that last winter of the war in Bastogne. I saw Europe from a truck with our gun towed behind. We'd named ours Joe Louis, and if somebody asked why, we'd say, "Because he was quick to put a German on his ass." I had eleven men in my crew, and we could get all six tons turned, loaded, and fired in five minutes flat. It was a dance we learned in Camp Gruber, Oklahoma, like that two-stepping the black folks did out west. We fought our way through France and into the Ardennes Forest, and in the winter of 1944, we took our place in that line of American guns, eighty-five miles' worth.

Big-gun fighting was a different kind of war. From that far away, I heard the battle before I saw it. The boom of howitzers had become a sweet sound to me. Our guns talked back to Hitler, getting the last word in when we put our shells on a man's head. It was a certain kind of screaming, outgoing fire, that told us that our lines were still holding.

But by December, so close to Christmas to have me thinking about home, the Germans had made it through the lines. "The Bulge" was what they called it. The Nazis had gathered a quarter million men in the woods. Coming at us that fast, the big guns couldn't do much. Batteries A, B, and D were ordered to retreat and make a new line ten miles back. The four guns of Battery C stayed behind to cover us. When they followed, we planned to do the same and cover them. Each rumble of their guns was good news that told us they were still fighting. The quiet told us they'd been overrun.

People talk about peace and quiet like they're kindred. The Ardennes Forest was the quietest place I'd ever known, and quiet was where the SS waited for us. Quiet was where those boys from Battery C ended up. I learned that quiet was not really quiet at all. It's the sound of friends tortured and dying too far away for anybody to hear. I prayed for them the same thing I'd prayed for myself. I hoped to die quickly and that whatever cut through me came like lightning without enough time for me to shake my head.

But I knew better when we saw the bodies of the eleven men who died at Wereth. The townspeople said a family had hidden them in their barn, but a neighbor had told the SS. The eleven soldiers, not a gun among them, did what they were taught and gave themselves up for surrender. The Nazis marched them toward a field, and that was the last the people in Wereth saw of them.

When the spring came and the snow thawed, we saw the ugly show the Germans had made of the killing. The folk said it had just looked like another mound in the snow. A drift, or a gun position covered over by the winter. When we heard about the bodies, we drove as fast as we could. An army chaplain looked for tags so he would know what name to call the men when he prayed. When I saw the bodies, I couldn't even close my eyes to pray on them, because I searched their faces, trying to recognize one friend from the other.

The Germans had taken their time, bayoneting them and cutting off fingers. Those spared the knife were beaten. Maybe the marks had come from rifle butts or boots, but whatever the weapon was, they'd struck them over and over. My mind filled up with that sickest kind of wondering, thinking about who had to be the first to feel it coming down. I wondered who was the last and had to see the rest die before he did.

I had been around my kin out in the country, and I had seen enough hog killing to know the propriety of such things. The particular way that we got quiet when the knife went in, because hog or not, it was still blood.

Two of the dead, George Davis and William Pritchett, came from Alabama. George talked about Montgomery like it was a country boy's metropolis. I told them they ought to visit when we got home. George said, "If I go back." At first I thought he was talking about dying, but he was talking about the opposite, living like a man who could go where he pleased. He thought about Detroit, New York maybe.

"Can't say for sure," he told me. "At least not yet, but somewhere."

Standing in that field, I tried so hard to remember their

voices, but all I could hear was that wartime quiet, how the world sounded to a dead man's ears. My mind always went back to the worst of it. Victory had not been enough, and neither had the time that passed. They were resting beneath the crosses in the Henri Cemetery, but I still saw them in that mud.

So when I saw that man jump onto the Empire Theater's stage, heard the weight of his pipe on that hardwood, and then saw him swing for Nat Cole's skull, I thought of other friends ambushed by men who'd been hiding and waiting. The dead quiet that came over that room when Nat Cole stopped the music was enough to stop my heart. And then came the ruckus and the screaming and me right in the middle of it. All I did was stand between a friend and his trouble.

My lawyer wore an Air Medal on his chest and one of those Tuscaloosa bow ties worn by the courthouse crowd. Johnson was his name, and he called me Sergeant Weary. He looked at a man in the back of the room. Johnson had a look on his young face like he himself was scared of getting put on that prison jitney with me.

"Attorney general's here, and, well—" he told me in a grave sort of whispering. "Seems like they want to make a show of it. They gave the other man three years."

I figured I might get thirty days' labor, but if the white boy got three years, then, Lord. When the months in my mind turned to years, the chain between my feet got twice as narrow, because balancing was all that I could manage. I put my knuckles on the corner of that table and tried to breathe and swallow. No wind wanted to come into me, and that jailhouse breakfast was about ready to come back up.

"How many they got in mind for me?"

"Like I said. Seems like they want to—"

He was being so careful with the bad news, which made it all the worse.

"The state's attorney," he said, nodding toward the man at the table across from us, a Bronze Star on his lapel, "he wants to give you ten years."

He laid it out. Inciting a riot. Five years. Aggravated assault. Three years. Reckless endangerment. Two years. Consecutive terms that added up to ten. I had turned twenty-six years old in a field in Belgium, two weeks after V-E Day. I would turn thirty-six, if I made it, in Kilby Prison. The number got my head to shaking inside and out.

"I need to fight it, then," I told him.

"Sergeant Weary, I'd be doing you a disservice if I let you in front of a Ripley Street jury. They'll give you twenty years just as sure as I'm standing here."

The lawyer said he couldn't keep me out of Kilby, but he said he could save me some years if I took his advice. If the judge asked me a question, I should say "Yes, sir" or "No, sir." Don't say a word unless His Honor invited me to. *Invited.* I had heard the story of a boy who had talked after the judge told him not to speak, and he got an extra year for every word. So I stood in the middle of all that quiet, waiting for His Honor to say how many years he was taking from me.

"Son," the judge said. In the wrong man's mouth, that word came at me like venom. "Son, you got anything to say for yourself?"

"No, sir." Calling that man "sir" was one of the biggest lies I've ever told.

After he took those years, that judge kept on talking, about honor and service and whatnot. But my ears were filled with my wartime hearing, that ringing that came in the middle of everything I heard. Some days all I heard was that thin, sharp sound that was like something drilling a little deeper into my ear each time. It was on account of my gun, six tons' worth that I had learned to use like a razor. Some called that sound an affliction, but I had learned to love it, because that was the sound of me killing men, Germans, hell-bent on doing to me what that judge had done.

I didn't know what came of that howitzer, but it was probably being dragged down a street somewhere on Armistice Day. I was unarmed when I jumped onto that stage. It was a fair fight with me standing between a friend and his trouble. When that judge took my years, all my hands could do was keep shaking, not from fear, but from all the fight that was still in me with nowhere to go.

Chapter 4

They didn't waste any time. I was on a work gang the day after I got off the prison jitney. That first morning they put me on a crew with seven other men, opened the west gate, and marched us to a patch of woods near Gunter Air Base. I had heard somebody say we were going to pull weeds, kudzu. The prison quartermaster handed me a shovel with one edge sharpened for chopping. When he put it in my hands, I thought the same thing any man would. How many times could I hit the jailers around me—quartermaster, guards—before the rest of them got those shotguns around? It was all that I could do to just keep my head this side of right, so I calmed myself, took my shovel, and got in line.

The two trusties, Uly and Polk, wore vertical stripes, different from ours. Their leg guards, strips of tin bolted to rawhide, rattled when they walked, and that was the cadence we walked to. They carried their machetes on their shoulders, and we did the same with whatever we had, spades, saws, and knotted coils of rope. We marched, four by two, past a pair of mile markers to reach the field. Once we had hiked knee-deep into the kudzu, Uly and Polk staked off about ten square yards, and we cut the vine back to the crown and then got to work on the root.

A full-grown stalk is as thick as my arm, and strong enough to snap a spade handle. It took a sharp end on something heavy to get through the gristle of a full-grown vine. Kudzu doesn't grow in the winter, and we had to get a head start before the vine started running after the spring rains. A new shoot could run a foot in a day. If a patch of Alabama got covered in kudzu, people who lived on it just moved on. It wasn't worth the time or the money to clear the land. For us it was different. We were prisoners clearing government land; as far as time, I had ten years, and some of the men on my crew would die in Kilby.

Uly worked his machete like his old hands had never touched anything else. My job was to dig around the crown. Uly stood beside me, looking into the hole like it went somewhere.

"Don't split that root, son. All it does is make two vines instead of one." His words came through his chewing and spitting the juice of the kudzu leaves he kept in his jaw.

Once I got enough room underneath, I lifted and I'll be damned if that root didn't feel stone heavy. With

enough of the crown lifted and that top bit of root showing, Polk looped a rope through the tangles, and all the
men grabbed hold of a knot and worked their feet into a
good hold on an open bit of ground or a net of weed thick
enough for balance. Uly called out "Ready, ready," and
he waited for us to say the same. When we got the next
call, we leaned our weight in one direction and pulled that
rope, over and again, each tug pulling another inch of
root, knowing more would sprout in the spring. Some of
those roots were twice as long as any man. I pulled with
everything in me, leaning so far back until I was damn
near sideways, every bit of muscle praying that the root
would give before I did.

My war gun was heavy but it sat on carriage wheels
with a well-oiled axle. It was meant for moving, but kudzu
was not. When I pulled on the worst of the crowns, I wondered if somebody was on the underside of the world tug-
ging the other way. Maybe hell was somebody else's Kilby,
and the dead had their own fields for toiling where their
devils smiled down on them just like the guards did on us.

The weed was too deep for running, so they left us un-
chained. Two guards watched the eight of us, with shotguns full of double-aught on their shoulders and .44s at
their sides. A man might end his prison time with a bullet
in his back if he tried to run or a shot to his chest if he
squared up to fight. I had to stop thinking about doing

either. Work was all I had to keep me from losing my right mind, so I put everything into the tangled-up vine in front of me.

"Hey, Showstopper, what the hell's wrong with you?" Polk was bent next to me talking in that hard whisper, tapping his blade on the buckets nestled in the weed.

"You fill ten today, they'll want twenty tomorrow. Ain't no prize for pulling kudzu crown," he said.

"Hell yes there is," Uly said. "Prize for pulling crown is more crown."

"Need something to put my mind on, that's all."

"What they give you, ten years? Well, hell, you want some backbone left when you get out."

"Ten years?" Uly said. He looked at Polk then. "That's all they give Showstopper? Need to call your ass Lucky."

They spoke to me without straightening their backs. For a second I forgot where I was and stood up to talk. They gave me that headshake and moan that told me I had done wrong.

"Keep low when you talk," Polk said. "Captain see you talk, he might think you don't have enough work. Lord knows we got plenty."

Polk told me he had come out of Chambers County and was kin to Joe Louis. But everybody I'd ever met from that corner of Alabama claimed to have some of that blood. Polk said he was raised in the boys' camp at Mount Meigs, and he told me he was over there with Satchel Paige. It couldn't have been true, because the years didn't line up. That gray hair in Polk's head had me thinking he was older than he was, closer to my father's age than mine.

"Figure I'm thirty or roundabouts," he said.

The hard living had pushed Polk's face closer to the bone, and the work left the muscle thin and twisted. Since the place had no mirrors, it would be years until I saw my face again. I saw what the future looked like on the faces of the men all around.

Polk was half Uly's age, but he was a trusty boss because he knew how the place worked. We didn't say anything to the guards outside of yes, no, sir, and boss. He spoke for us all.

"Hey, boss. How 'bout this one? Got the boys pulling good and well today. Good and well."

We had twenty yards of kudzu between us and the guards, so he yelled and held up a just-pulled root like it was a channel catfish. Polk worked that shine talk just like he worked that machete. He had learned to put on a show for the guards. Uly didn't say much, just nodded mostly, like everything Polk said needed a second.

It hurt me to hear it, worse than the ringing in my ears that still came and went. Men did that "yes sir, boss" talk and loved it. Polk did it to make the work go faster, because the trusted men got the sharpest tools. Our bosses had all kinds of ways to shame a man. I would learn that in time. A man who stared too long, or spoke out of turn, or even looked like he was about to, got the worst of it. The quartermaster might hand him something made with splintered wood and twisted iron.

Polk said something to make them laugh, and before they finished, he had his back to them again, his smile dropped back to nothing. I looked up to watch the two guards, carrying on, warming themselves around the barrel where the burning root crackled.

"You need to stare, stare at that shovel," Polk said.

My face showed too much. It always had. I was in a place where it might do me harm. Maybe the guards would know where my head was, swinging a shovel at them instead.

"I keep something on my mind when I'm out here. Something I saw back home. An undersheriff got kicked by a horse he wanted to ride in the parade. He the one threw me in jail that first time. That horse kicked his ass in front of everybody that side of Buckaloo Mountain. See, I think about something to bring a smile to my face, that way I don't have to kill somebody, my own self included. You—you ought to think about them ten crackers you whipped with a bugle. That's what it was, right?"

For a second I felt that microphone's steel in my hand, but I had nothing but the wood and knots on that handle. I figured I'd let my mind make something new.

"Trombone. That's what it was. "

"Valve or slide?"

"Both. One in each hand."

Uly looked over smiling then, letting a line of that kudzu spit fly.

"See there, Polk. Showstopper was switch-hitting like one of them Black Barons."

Polk looked over at the guards, the fire too low in the barrel to see much flame. They'd be looking over again soon, barking this and that, calling us something worse than what they'd called us before, and that would start that burning inside me, a feeling worse than the aching that had spread from my back, everyplace except my hands and feet, too cold from that winter and thin clothes to feel anything but the shovel and the ground.

Folks were meant to feel a certain way on Friday evenings, when a week of working was behind them. But Fridays in Kilby mattered for the worst reason. That was execution day. As we marched along the roadside, cars rolled past with plates from the wiregrass, the foothills, and the delta. Some of the cars had the lights on top and others just a county seal, but they were district attorneys and sheriffs ready to watch their man take his turn in the electric chair. They called it Yellow Mama, but the prisoners did not, because the kind of man to name something like that was the kind who'd never have to take his turn in the seat.

The executions started at five o'clock, and some days they killed two or three, always on the hour. We knew the chair was hot when the lights blinked once, twice, or maybe three times if the first jolt didn't finish a man. Otherwise they kept the lights on in the death house, to make a point that didn't really need making. They didn't have but one light switch for a man on the row. Preachers used to say that we know neither the day nor the hour, but a death house man knew both. Kilby had turned that bit of scripture into a lie.

We marched past the cemetery, where the graveyard crew boiled water for the unclaimed bodies. Because that winter ground was so hard, they poured steaming buckets over the cemetery dirt before they shoveled. Three gurneys lined the death house wall. Uly told me that when it was cold enough for the bodies to keep, they'd leave them out on Friday and Saturday, covered under denim blankets until the funeral on Sunday morning. That was the day for our personal business—visitors, mail call, or getting buried.

The guards went only as far as the gatehouse, so we marched to the cell block on our own. We had plenty of people watching. The tower guards kept an eye out and so, too, did the visitors on the main house balconies waiting for the executions. We were part of the same show, marching with our lines as sharp as the airmen on the parade grounds over at Gunter Air Base. The trusties had the big house looking its best. The camellias were blooming, and I thought the same thing I always thought when I saw them, that winter was the wrong time for flowers and Kilby was the wrong place.

I saw something on my first Friday that I'd not seen in the days before it. When we got close to the death house, a few of the men slipped their rags from their pockets and tied them around their necks. They'd dipped those rags in kerosene we used for root burning, so the smell was still strong in their noses as we marched those last few yards to our block. Uly started on a fresh chaw of kudzu, rolling a few bits of torn leaves and a thick slice of root. Before we started to walk, he had told me to gather up the same, so I chewed on mine as well.

He had told me why, so I could be ready on that first walk and every one after. The bitters of the leaves and the starch of the root were enough to keep my stomach still when we walked past the chamber. Smokestacks lined the Kilby roof, and we all knew which one carried the air from the chair room. When that wind hit us, we couldn't help but know what was mixed in it, the last bit of breathing a man did when they strapped him in, and after that, the warm smell of his smoke.

Whenever I saw the lights blinking, I hoped he died on his first shot so he wouldn't have to live through his burning. The men in my crew stopped talking then, because whether we knew the dying man or not, it was only decent to be quiet if we couldn't be still. Polk stopped calling the cadence and just let the rustle of his leg guards keep the time.

Chapter 5

On that first time Warden Duggan stood before us, those fresh off the bus from Ripley Street jail, he said that a man had to get used to his time inside, so we would have no visitors for sixty days. By the time I sat in that visiting room waiting for Mattie, the January cold was blowing in from every which way. I had prayed I would never feel another winter like the one I'd had in Belgium the year before, but I had found one worse than Europe a few miles from home.

The visiting room was in the old denim factory. Blue lint still covered the rafters, and webs of it came down, shaken loose by the birds that nested up there. I could tell a man who'd just come from seeing his people, because the blue dust colored his shoulders.

The cold and my nerves together had set my hands to shaking, so I did all I could to calm myself, or to look calm at least. A man couldn't show such things inside Kilby's walls, so I put my shaking hands tight against the plywood of the visiting stall. My feet had the worst of it, though. The cardboard soles of the brogans couldn't do much to keep me warm. But the cold killed the stench at least. When they'd handed me those shoes, they still smelled like the last man's feet.

I did all I could to look my best. I gave the laundry trusty a month's tobacco rations and a handful of starch clay I'd brought in from the road. He said he'd mix the starch with water and soak my collar before he put the iron on it. I wanted to make my creases right and bring a little bit of order to myself. As for my face, I had to make do. Regulations said a Kilby man had to be clean-shaven, but we weren't allowed to use razors. All I had was a wooden spatula, lye, and whatever I could find to cool the burn. No matter if we cut the lye with potato or mashed kudzu root, the paste took off as much skin as it did hair, and the slick scars on a man's face stayed with him. With no glass mirror, just a scratched bit of metal nailed to the wall, I shaved blind and trusted the sting to tell me my face was clean.

We got one shower a week, and a man expecting visitors took it on Saturday, trying to scrub off six days of funk in that two minutes between the water bells they rang. I used that same lye soap I shaved with. Even getting clean, cold water or not, felt like burning.

When Mattie walked in, I wanted to stand. Notions of what was right and proper, what a man would do out of courtesy or love, had to be forgotten in favor of the rules. I couldn't raise a hand or leave my seat in the visitors' room, so I lifted my head and came as close to a smile as I could.

She said my name, but it was more breath than voice.

Seeing Mattie sitting across from me was a new kind of pain. She put on a good face for me, but she clinched her hands so tight that the veins kept rolling. With all of that straining in her smile, she surely felt like I did every hour, Kilby troubling me down to the root.

She put her hands along the edge of the chicken wire, as much of a touch as they would let us have. With the gauge of the mesh as tight as it was, we could barely find space that didn't have a piece of that wire on our fingertips.

"We're doing everything to get you home," she said, pushing a little harder.

"Just wanted to take you to a show. All I wanted."

"When we get you out of here, we'll go somewhere. Maybe we'll stay for good."

When she talked about getting me out, I smiled because I loved her and everything she was doing for me. But I knew full well nothing would open the Kilby gate before I'd done every day of my time.

"And you? What about you?" I asked her.

I knew the answer. I could see the strain in her face, and

the throbbing in her temple. That's what that prison did to anybody sitting where she was. Like everyone on that side of the visiting stalls, she wanted to be a rock. But a rock could do only so much. We had a prison yard full, and men spent their days busting them down to gravel.

"I'm holding on. Thinking about getting you home," she said. "Dr. Burk gave me the rest of the term off. She wrote letters trying to get some lawyers down here. She met Charles Houston when he was down here for the Scottsboro trial. I wrote to William Lewis in Washington. He worked for President Roosevelt. Lots of people are working to get you out."

I knew all about the Scottsboro Boys, and thinking about them made things worse. People had come from all over to help the nine of them, sent to prison on a bald-faced lie. One of them was still on my tier. His face was scarred where they'd shot him when he tried to escape. They couldn't give that man his years back, and they couldn't give him his right mind when Kilby broke him.

"They've been throwing soldiers in jail all over. People are talking, trying to get something done about it. We have good lawyers working. Doing all we can."

That smile she gave me then. Something pieced back together.

"Tell them I said thank you," I said.

"You don't have to thank anybody. You saved a man."

The trembling in her fingertips had been calm for a while, and Mattie's hands were like every other woman's in that place, fingers pressed hard against the wire trying to squeeze what they could through. The families were too practiced in coming to Kilby on a Sunday morning, and they knew that place as well as they knew their front rooms and church pews, where they should have been come Sunday.

"They can't do this."

"They already did, baby. I love you for fighting for me, but you need to get ready for them saying no. When they give a man ten years, they don't go back on it."

I hated to watch her drop her head then, because I knew our time was short. Her fingers rolled against mine, and some of the ink remained from her fingerprinting, treating her like she was locked up, too.

"Couple days before the show. You were talking about going to Oakland and spending a little time with your sister after she had the baby."

She was silent for a moment, looking away. A few months had passed since that talk, but it seemed like so much time and California so far away. The prison walls and a fence line made it only that much farther.

"What'd they name the baby?"

"Joshua. Just made a month old."

"He's got a big head on him like his pop?"

"He'll grow into his head, I'm sure."

"His pop's twenty-five, and he still hasn't grown into his yet."

She had easiness in her face, and I wanted to remember it. I had nothing but dead years between right then and 1955.

"You just need to go and see your people. Get your mind off this for a while at least. Get on a train and see that baby. It does me good to know you're out in the world with your folks."

"I can't get my mind off this. Not with you in here."

"You still need to go see your people. Go back to work. Otherwise Kilby might take your years, too. You don't owe the state of Alabama any time. They got me for that."

"Part of me wishes you'd killed him. We could have gotten you in a car and taken you somewhere."

"Never been the type to run. You neither." It was hard to talk to her without seeing things as they should have been. My mind went back and forth between that and what was around me.

"Go out there and hold that baby. Your sister could use a little rest."

"They do as they please," she said, rocking.

"Always have. But you— Go see your people and send my love. We'll talk when you get home."

The fellow in the stall next to me wore one of those sad

little wedding rings the men made. Some dried piece of weed twisted around his finger. He couldn't have anything real, because the guards might take it, say it was a weapon. Some men had married the women sitting across from them in ceremonies at the little jailhouse church in the pine grove. That kind of marriage turned them all into widows. It was no kind of life. Mattie might as well be sitting by my headstone at Lincoln Cemetery. And what could I give her but empty years, a marriage on some old stools in the jailhouse visiting room. It could not be.

Mattie and I had been married once.

On a leave weekend from Camp Gruber, I met her at a boardinghouse in Muskogee. The sign on the front desk said they rented only to married folks, but all the soldiers knew they didn't ask for papers. It was wartime, and our uniforms were license enough. The man at the front desk turned the book around and read the name like he was Saint Peter.

"Mr. and Mrs. Nathaniel Weary. Welcome to Muskogee," he said, and hearing it out loud made it sound closer to being true.

When we made it upstairs, Mattie took a bottle of what I smelled on her neck and sprayed it in that little room. The loving I had done as a young man had come in little stolen places, listening for the sound of some girl's momma and daddy who might open a bedroom door. There was all that stealing time, biting my lip or hiding the sounds that wanted to bubble out with the rest of it. In that hotel, we had a good taste of full-grown loving behind a locked door in a good and wide bed. When we talked afterward, with Mattie's cheek close to my chest, we didn't need our voices, because the words went straight into skin. As long as I made it home from the war, that was how it would always be.

Behind the Kilby church stood four shacks in a row. If a prisoner was a good worker, and if the warden gave permission, a man and his wife could have a conjugal visit, half an hour twice a year. I spent a day on a crew that cleaned the pine straw from the shacks' roofs. Each building had two rooms, one where the guard sat and one with a small bed. The doorway had no door, and the windows had no draperies. They rationed husbands and wives to one another, turned what was private into a shame. Any guard strolling by could get an eyeful of what was meant to be hidden. And, Lord, did they stroll. A trusty told me, "You get used to it after a while. Can't do nothing else if it's all you got."

They led the prisoners from the Sunday visiting room to the church. I was close enough to the parking lot to see Mattie and my sister, who had driven her. I was too far away to see their eyes and faces, but they were close enough to be in the same piece of shadow. And Mattie rested her head on Marie's shoulder, and that was the last I saw of them before I walked through that church door.

I had no choice but to sit in that prison sanctuary, but I did most of my churching in my head. I prayed that Mattie would be happy in her life without me, and I prayed that she would understand when I told her not to come back. When I stopped sending letters. I wouldn't send any more dead man's words, talking about a love I couldn't bring to her door. I couldn't be anybody's man but Kilby's.

Chapter 6

E very other Sunday. Fifteen minutes and no more. I was
allowed one visitor at a time. That was all I got of my
family for nine years and seven months. It was the third
Sunday in June, and I walked into the visiting room, looking for my brother sitting in the stall. A stranger sat in his
place. When I'd walked across the yard from my block, I'd
seen Dane's cab turn off the road, so he must have driven
the man who was watching me as I walked to my seat.

It had been seven years since my last visit from a
stranger, the last of the lawyers who had tried mightily.
After that I told my family to understand that hope had no
place in Kilby. I no longer lived for the day when I would
go free. I lived for the odd Sunday when I could see my
people, if only through the rusted-out wires. If prison had
taught me anything, it was to let my face say nothing. So
the stranger did not see my disappointment. I had learned
to stop craving anything from the world, except for my

people. With him in my brother's place, it would be another thirteen days before I saw family again.

This stranger had a mark across his forehead left from
a hat he wore a little bit cocked. He had a brand-new shave.
That was something I missed, living someplace where I
could lean back, close my eyes, and trust a man to put a
razor to my neck.

"Morning, Mr. Weary. Augustine Tate. They call me
Skip."

He rolled his hands along the counter like they held an
offering. Some fingers were straighter than others, and
that, along with the line of his nose, told me that he had
been a fighter. From the gray and wrinkles he carried
along his head and his face, it seemed that his fighting
days were years behind.

I nodded, but I said nothing, figuring whatever he had
to say he'd get to.

"Sorry to take your family time, but I came to talk business."

"I got no business."

"Well, Mr. Weary—"

"Don't call me mister. No good getting used to it in
here."

"No, sir. I'll call you Mr. Weary. I owe you that much.
Wasn't for you I wouldn't have a job. See, I work for Nat
Cole. He sent me to talk to you."

I had not heard that name in so long. Nat had sent letters, asking about lawyers and legal bills and whatnot.
He was like all the rest of the folks who meant well and
thought that something could be done. I told my people to
tell him no. He didn't owe me a thing. All he did was mind
his business.

"Wasn't for you, I might not have a job," he said. "I'm his
driver and his bodyguard."

"You can't do much guarding sitting right here."

"You're right, Mr. Weary. We're thinking ahead, getting
something lined up for a few months from now. He needs
to have one more man he can trust, and your name's top
of his list."

"Long way to come to hire a man."

"A man we can be certain of. Every Negro singer in
America knows what happened to Nat Cole in Alabama.
They started hiring prizefighters and gangsters and ex-
cons to do what you did. Stand in there if the time comes.
You put more folk to work than Roosevelt."

He had meant it as humor. But those reflexes, the laughing and smiling, I didn't use much anymore. So all I could
muster was a nod.

"The thing is, Mr. Weary—"

"Just call me Weary."

"Weary, you can pay an army of fighters and the like,
but you never really know what somebody's liable to do

until it's time. Except for you, of course. We know exactly what Nathaniel Weary will do."

"Like I said, I did what I had to."

"No. You could have watched him get his head knocked in."

The sound of a guard turning a window crank interrupted us. The blue cobwebs fell, and I would have thought that during my time inside the last of it would have rained down already. Some of the dust fell on Augustine Tate, who wore the clothes meant for better places, like the Los Angeles he spoke about, where looking respectable meant something. I could not see myself in Los Angeles, because my eyes had dimmed to such things.

"You can tell Nat that me being in here ain't his doing. Appreciate the gesture but—"

"It ain't just gratitude behind all this, Weary. Nat's got a television show that starts this fall. They wanted to whale on him for being onstage, imagine when he's sitting in everybody's living room? He sent me to make an offer, and to listen to you say yes."

"I got a job waiting for me here."

"I talked to your brother. Told me an ex-con can't get a taxi shield. Best you can do is be some shade-tree mechanic."

"I don't need a license to pump gas."

The look on his face then. Like he'd just heard the sorriest thing a man could say, but I didn't care. I had to stop yearning for the world. There was no place left for ambition. So after all those hollowed-out years, pumping gas in a filling station five miles from Kilby was dream enough. It was damn near heaven.

"You got better waiting for you, Weary."

"Better than prison? Tell me what ain't."

"You're right. If I was in here, suspect I'd feel the same."

He took two cigarettes from his shirt pocket, lifted them in his hand as he looked toward the guard. The screw walked over.

"Hope you got a third one," I told him. "Got to pay your tithes in here."

Skip turned toward him, and the guard motioned for him to lay them on the countertop. He looked back at me and shrugged. Pulled one more cigarette so the guard got his, too.

"Tithes my ass," he said, low enough for me to hear. "This here is usury. The Lord only takes ten percent."

He smiled then, and passed a lit cigarette through the wire.

"You didn't ask how much money you'll be making, Weary."

"Seems I didn't."

"Three hundred dollars a week. Once the TV money comes in probably more. It won't give years back to you, but it's something. Put some miles between you and Alabama. See a little piece of the world."

The tobacco was sweet and strong. I was used to smoking what came from the prison farm at Limestone. No sooner than that good tobacco went through me, I could feel the possibilities. An old part of my mind had opened once again. Skip spoke of life in Los Angeles. While he talked my mind went there. I saw myself on unknown streets, better than that yard dust I walked across every day.

The guard had lit his cigarette, and no sooner than he'd filled his lungs, he emptied them, coughing behind us. I was facing him, and knew better than to look his way. Skip smiled.

"Cuban squares. Stronger than most. Smoke got the drop on him."

I didn't nod or smile. I just let it be one of those agreed-upon things without a word or gesture. Shaming a guard came at a cost, and my time was too short for such.

"Just so you know, Weary. This wasn't automatic. I told Nat I'd take a look. Told him maybe Kilby got the best of you. But I can see that ain't the case."

Truth be told, I had damn near lost my mind more than once. It was so easy for my mind to find better places, but coming back to this world was harder each time.

"I don't know a thing about Los Angeles."

"You didn't know anything about killing Nazis, and that worked out all right."

He had offered a job with the most famous Negro in America. Jackie Robinson had retired, and every team had at least one of us. The television networks had none. Being famous had a cost for Nat Cole. A bullet through a window. The IRS trying to take his house. All manner of things in the mailbox. Skip had begun to walk the Coles' property at night, and he needed a day man to take on the driving.

He talked with his hands and needed more room than he had. He drove home each point with his finger into the plywood tabletop. Though his voice barely moved above a whisper, his hands made up for it. Every so often, he made fists. Always the left hand first and then the right.

"I imagine the world's going to be strange to you anyhow. Might as well let it be strange somewhere new. You got a friend in Los Angeles looking out for you. And in a few months you'll be looking out for him in return. Think it over."

"No," I told him. "I did all my thinking just now. Tell him I said thank you and yes."

That was the first time I had said such—thank you and yes—and meant it in all those years. I said as much to the guards all the time. *Yes, sir. Thank you, sir.* But it was no different than the knife I kept hidden sideways beneath my belt. A tool to keep living, even if life in there wasn't about much.

"Just got one more question. Like I said, everybody heard about the fellow who whipped the man who tried to whip Nat Cole. But, you know people tell a good story and sometimes they add their own gravy. So you never know how it happened. What kind of horn did you beat that man with? Some said a trumpet, and some say a trombone."

"I used a microphone."

"I asked Nat, and he wouldn't say. Said you never correct somebody's legend."

Skip rose to leave. He was a good six inches taller than me. Splinters of plywood had caught in his gabardine, and he brushed them to the floor with the ash and dust.

"What's Nat riding in?" I asked.

"Cadillac limousine. Until they come up with something better."

As Skip fell in with the line of leaving visitors, I allowed myself to see a better future. Pumping octane at the station my sister and brother-in-law owned was too humble. I saw myself driving through Los Angeles in a car longer than my cell, and it had already become real.

As soon as my visiting time was through, I walked across the yard to the church. My brother stood by his cab, looking at me. I moved slowly, trying to hold on to my freest minutes as long as I could. We were not allowed to wave at anyone beyond the fence line. The guards in the tower might think we were signaling, a prison break in the works, and that was reason enough to shoot somebody dead. In five months the gate would open for me to leave that place. Augustine Tate had given me a taste of the free-side world. When I closed my eyes in that prison church, I paid no mind to the chaplain, I took a little trip to the place that waited for me when I got out.

Chapter 7

Montgomery

DAY OF THE SHOW
1:15 P.M.

I wondered how many times I could come back to Alabama before I had to start calling it something other than home. Home from war and home from prison. A year in Los Angeles changed everything, or at least I wanted it to. I had a house on Seventy-Fourth Street in Los Angeles, and for that week I'd been back in Montgomery, I'd found my rest in a third-floor suite at the Centennial Hotel. My hotel room was two floors above the cabstand I'd pretty much grown up in. I had spent as many hours there as I had spent at my house. A hotel room was a place for strangers, and that's what I felt like. Maybe that was as it should be, so I could do the day's work and get gone.

My brother and sister had offered me a place to stay,

but they had families of their own. Besides, I wanted space and quiet to get everything ready for the show. Part of me, most of me, was fine with hotel living. With that corner room view on top of Centennial Hill, I saw my hometown as newcomers and travelers did, from the windows of a rented room.

I had reserved three of the four corner suites for the show. Each was named for the views it offered, College Hill, Riverside, Capitol Heights, and Centennial. Nat got College Hill, the southeast corner facing Bama State with its treetops and the copper dome on the bell tower. Skip took Centennial, the same one they'd given him when he visited me at Kilby. I stayed in the Riverside Suite, and it was nice enough. The best part was the sturdy walls that kept the room so quiet that the door knock I heard sounded more like a rumble.

"Good afternoon, Mr. Weary."

Mrs. Varner stood there holding one of the hotel trays. I couldn't get used to her calling me Mr. Weary, because she'd been at the hotel since it opened and had known me all of my years. She had insisted though. We were both professionals, she'd told me, and reminded me that I was grown, half as long as she'd been grown, but grown just the same.

"I heard our secret guest has arrived safely."

"Yes, ma'am. We got him situated in his room."

"I wanted to greet him at the door. You said not to make a big show out of him coming, but it is a big show."

"Yes, ma'am. But it'll be even bigger if we save the surprise until the time's right."

"And when will that be?"

"His name goes on the marquee at three o'clock when the ticket window opens. Mr. Worthy will make an announcement on the radio at four."

"It's a strange plan, but it's yours and we'll follow. I must say, I do like to see somebody with a plan in charge. Heart after my own. You might be tired of me saying so."

"No ma'am. Not at all."

She set the tray on the table between the high-back chairs in the corner. She put it down gingerly, but the weight of it still rattled the tea set and the water glasses already there.

"We got something for Mr. Cole."

She leaned and picked up the edges of the cloth to show me the bronze plaque. NATHANIEL ADAMS "KING" COLE SUITE. It took two lines to fit every word of that name, the one he was born with and the one just for show.

"The white hotels downtown have presidential suites and the like, even if no president saw fit to stay there. Mr. Cole is our biggest guest and he's home folk, and we can say in all honesty he laid his head across the hall there. We might as well let people know."

"He'll be happy to see it."

"I figure we'll make a little fuss and show it to him this afternoon. Put it on an easel upstairs in the ballroom. If it was up to me you'd have one right alongside his."

The bronze had been rubbed at the edges to give it a little gleam. Nat had a crown above his name just like the one on the spinning sign that had started every episode of his television show. Those signs had been made of balsa wood and painted to look like something more. Every prop was meant to fool you and look real, but they were all light enough to carry and cheap enough to throw away when the show was done. That plaque in the Centennial's hallway, on the door of the finest room, was meant to stay as long as the building did. Something heavy, bolted deep into the plaster and the frame.

"He'll try to be modest about it, but he'll appreciate you for doing as much."

Before she covered the plaque again, she rubbed the crown and letters with the corner of that cloth.

"Thought maybe you were busy with everything going on, but I wanted to make sure I visit with you before you go."

Those chairs were the same as the ones behind the desk in the cabstand. To see Mrs. Varner in one was to remember her visits with my mother. She'd bring two cups of something steaming, whatever the hour and season called for, and they would sit and talk when they had a bit of time.

"They told me at the front desk you're leaving us to-morrow. But as long as it's for something greener, I'll try not to get sad all over again. I always wish young folks well. I didn't get to say it to you last time, but I'm saying it now."

"I'm taking Nat to the airport in the morning, and then I'm heading back to Los Angeles."

"That's a good piece of driving. You got somebody to split it with you?"

"Just me, but I been out there and back on my own. I make my money driving, so the road's the best place for me."

She patted my hand one good time, and looked around the room. I kept it tidy, shoes lined along the baseboards and my hats stacked on the open shelf of the wardrobe.

"Catherine cleaned this floor today. I see she took care of everything like she was supposed to."

Miss Vee lifted the glasses that hung around her neck to look at the windowsills and the radiator, the places where the dust liked to hide. As simple as the hotel was, it was never less than tidy. She used to clean the place before she became day manager, her title embroidered on her jacket in maroon and silver. The glasses hung on a chain of stones in those same colors.

"It's impolite to ask what the man's like, because you

work for him and wouldn't dare tell his business. But I know it's nice working for Negroes."

Miss Vee was right. I had never worked for white folks, but I had been in the US Army and an Alabama prison. Working for my own felt more like kindred.

"I got to Montgomery when I was fourteen from down there in Lowndes," she said. "That was the last time I ever worked for white folks. Give me Negro strangers. New folks to greet every day."

Miss Vee worked the desk the day I checked in, and she gave me that hug that people do without speaking. Her quiet was as strong as somebody else's shout. It was the same with my mother's name. She had not once mentioned her during that week I had been in Montgomery, but I knew she would eventually. I had steeled myself, or at least thought I had.

"Your mama and I talked about what you'd do when you left here. I had told her New York or someplace. I knew that if I ever asked after you I'd hear good news."

I didn't see Miss Vee before I left for California, and maybe I'd been hiding from folks. No matter how I carried myself, it took a while to get loose of that Kilby feeling. People didn't ask me how I was doing and where I had been, they just hugged my neck or shook my hand too hard. I felt the pity in everybody's touch.

"I'm glad you left here, Nathaniel. Glad you came back, too."

She was my mother's friend, one of her best over so many years. She knew that I had to mourn my mother in prison, a place that hardly respected living, let alone death and grieving.

"When she died I was out there, Miss Vee. I can't get past it," I told her, and my voice didn't fail me. Tears stayed too low to spill over.

"Nobody expects you to, son. You're not out there now."

She left again then, and I was back in my quiet. It wasn't sound, but the place was plenty enough filled. Miss Vee and her people still sprinkled their mixture in the vacuum bag, a spoonful of nutmeg or chicory. Cinnamon. Satsuma and clementine peels when they were in season. All of that plus the baking soda they sprinkled on the carpets before they cleaned them. All of our steps across those floors stirred up something sweet. When I rubbed my feet on the carpet, I breathed it into my lungs. Holding in that good dust and trying to let go of all the rest.

I stepped out my door, and Skip stood down the hall on the pay phone, shuffling through the nickels in his palm. Once he finished his call, he dropped the handful of change back into his pocket and waved me over.

"Everything's set for when we get back to Chicago. New York on Thursday, then London Friday morning. Carlos had Nat booked through New Year's, but they sold every seat. Might add a few more shows. 'Twelve Nights of Nat Cole' or some such."

"He'll like some good news."

"He could sing about Christmas in July, and they'd still pay good money. I wonder if he ever gets tired of that song. But a hit record is a hit record."

"That's his money."

"Ours, too."

"Miss Vee left a plaque in my room. They're naming the suite for him. It's not sellout show news, but it'll be good for him to know."

"It's nice, I suspect, get your name on something. You see how they started busting up the sidewalk down on Hollywood Boulevard? Walk of fame, my ass. Got it looking like a cemetery with a bunch of headstones. Name on a room is different. People pay big money for a suite, so they might as well see somebody's name on it."

The windows faced High Street, and the Christmas displays had people stopped and looking. Gray's Electronics and Records had a display in the window, a fake fireplace with a flashing jukebox where the flames would have been. On the record covers in the window, singers wore red and green, and album titles were spelled out in letters the color of the tinsel and ribbon wrapped around the streetlights up and down the block.

"How's it feel, old man. Back in Montgomery?"

"It looks small. This hotel. The houses. The sidewalks look too narrow. Leaving changes everything."

"Didn't know what to think of this place when I came looking for you. When Nat sent me out here, that was the first time he'd ever told me about that show. I'd heard all kind of stories, but never from him. He told me he wanted to do right by you."

"He already did. I made more money in a year out there than I would have in five here. Hell, maybe ten."

"That's well and good, Weary. But still. His pride. With the show cancelled and all. If he puts some money in your hand, you can put up a little fuss, but then you fold it in your pocket. Just call it meantime money. Until he comes back to Los Angeles."

"How long?"

"Carlos might book New York when Nat comes back. The road's been better to him than television, so who knows."

"If he needs me when he comes back, that's fine. But he doesn't owe me."

"He knows that man was liable to kill him if not for you

whipping his ass. If he puts money in your hand, put it in your pocket."

He pointed out the window at the southbound bus that let out a dozen or so nurses at Saint Margaret's Hospital, the last stop for white riders before Centennial Hill.

"I think I figured out how to solve the bus problem down here. Double-decker busses. That way if anybody can't stand sitting next to you, they can carry their ass up the stairs."

"You can see about bringing one back from London."

"I'll look into it."

Skip took another handful of change and started to dial a new number, and he reminded me of his warning about a man's money and his pride.

"Take what he puts in your hand."

"Mr. Adams, it's Weary."

Whenever we knocked on Nat's door at any hotel, we used the name he checked in under, his middle name, in case somebody in the hallway overheard. The hours before a show need to be anonymous ones, so he had to be somebody else. Nat opened the door without showing himself, and closed the door behind me. He had changed out of his traveling suit, and he wore a red sweater and the round glasses he didn't like people to see him in.

"I know you don't care for surprises, so I'm telling you.

This suite's about to get a new name. Miss Vee made a plaque for you, with you being famous and all."

"Boy from Saint John Street with his name on the wall."

"About to be out front in a little while, too. They'll have you on the marquee and the radio after that. Then everybody'll know."

"All my time in show business, Weary, and this is a first. A show nobody knows about."

"Every other week you had a surprise guest, and folks loved it."

"Good for ratings, they told me. Right, too. Ratings were never my problem."

One of the property rooms at NBC held doors for all the shows. Offices, mansions, hospitals. Cardboard elevators. One door used for *The Nat King Cole Show* had a question mark, and he opened it to reveal mystery guests. In Montgomery Nat and I had been on the wrong end of a surprise that his attackers had kept secret until they were ready.

"You can't dwell. You said so yourself."

"Turns out I was wrong. I can dwell, but there's no future in it."

"Skip got good news about London. He wanted to tell you himself, but you and surprises."

"I'd bring you along if I could. I hope you know that."

"You got Skip looking out for you. You can hire somebody to drive when you get there."

"You've never been just a driver, Weary. Anyway, after this evening, you can call yourself a promoter. The world can always use a good one. I ended up in Los Angeles when one ran off with the money and left me stranded. I guess that worked out, so television shouldn't worry me like it does."

Nat had rearranged the furniture. The narrow table, no longer against the wall, was in front of the winged-back chair, turned into a workplace for the stack of staff pages. He'd made more room by moving the water pitcher and bowl and one of the lamps, placing them on the bottom shelf of the wardrobe. The red velvet chair's seat cushion was dimpled from the bit of sitting he'd done while he worked.

"Which way is it, the neighborhood?"

He asked as he stood facing the window with his hands on the back of the chair, rocking it on two legs while he looked at the Hill. I pointed toward Saint John Street, but we couldn't see any of the narrow shotgun houses, much lower than the trees. No landmarks outside of memory.

"My father's church?"

"On the west side. You can see the steeple. So many over there, it might be hard to tell which is which."

"I learned to play here. That piano at the house. One at First Baptist, too," he said. "Can hardly picture it, but this is where it was. I wonder if they changed out the pianos."

"We can take a ride and see if you want."

He didn't answer right off, his face had a look full of caution and maybe.

"What about the other one? The Empire piano. I'm sure it's right there still."

He didn't ask about the direction of the theater. If he saw it in his head the same way I saw it in mine, we didn't need a window or map to find it. Thinking about that place put me right in the middle of it again.

"Crazy thing is, as far as theaters go it's beautiful," he said. "Looks like the Palladium in London. A little bit smaller. One balcony instead of two. I wish the look of it was all I saw when I remembered it."

"Tonight you'll be upstairs. It'll be different."

He nodded, but there wasn't anything certain about it. Like he was making his head move, but his mind wasn't following.

"Sammy's singing 'Route 66' in his Vegas show. That's where he had that car crash. He said singing about a road he almost died on takes the sting out of driving on it. I tried to write one about Alabama, but nothing worked. Maybe coming back might do the trick."

He returned to the seat, the best and newest of the chairs in the building. When somebody came to that suite in a year or two and saw his name beside the door, they'd know that he'd sat there.

"I think about Montgomery and I don't hear any music.

I see a man with a pipe. You in prison. If I remember it like that, then I wonder if that's how the homefolk remember me."

"This time tomorrow all they'll remember is the show. You can get last time off your back."

"And yours?" he asked me.

"I let it go when I left here for California."

It was a lie, but a lie meant for good. It might help him to think that one of us had let go of that evening. Remembering put it out front again and all around, big and bright as that light that blinded Nat to the man rushing the stage.

The third-floor suites gave the same views as the ball-room, so the people listening and drinking could walk around the place and see the whole city. My suite looked down on the alley where my brother's car was, back from his midday runs. His cab sat at the end of the line. A new paint job had the orange and the checkers shining, but it was the same car he'd driven me to the bus station in when I was off to the army, the same car he'd taken me and Mattie to the Empire in, the one he drove Skip out to Kilby to meet me in.

Every once in a while when I was out on the road crew, I saw a bright car on the highway. To see it was to dream about leaving. To have seen a spot of orange out on the highway fooled my heart into gladness, and sometimes I'd let my mind go along. And then the day finally came.

Chapter 8

The day they let me out of Kilby, Dane drove me home with one hand on the wheel and the other on my shoulder. When we took the first turn out of the parking lot and through the gate, he held on like I was liable to fly through the window and tumble back inside again.

"You look good," he said. And for good measure he said it twice more.

The access road curled through a pine grove before it hit the highway, so I had to see the prison once more as the road wrapped around the grounds and circled back toward Montgomery. I looked one last time, and let those walls and towers get small until I could close my eyes and let that be the end of Kilby.

By the time we got to Wetumpka Road, Dane finally let me loose and stretched his free hand along the seat behind me. He had let his beard grow in again. Every so often he'd shave and show up at the prison looking like he was a teenager. Dane was a junior in high school when I went to war, and he had become grown in my absence. He had a picture of Eleanor and the kids pinned to the driver's side visor. That evening, I would meet my niece and nephew for the first time.

Yes I was free, but I was not home. Kilby was inside of Montgomery proper, so during those ten years I had never left my city. I didn't start to feel at home until we reached Jackson and High and the checkerboard paint of the cabstand. Most days my mother kept the window open so she could call the next driver to get a fare. Among the things I had hoped for in vain was that one day I would walk in and see her where she had always been, running the office, chatting with Miss Vee or whoever was in the seats across from her desk.

I started saying good-bye to my mother and father the day I got drafted, and I didn't stop until the bus to basic training was too far gone for me to see them. My leaving didn't have a bit of surprise in it. The last thing my mother said to me the night I went to Nat's show was that I looked nice and not to keep Mattie waiting, which I never did, but she told me just the same. The night I left for the show, the words were too quick. We spoke like people who expected to see each other again in a few hours' time.

It had come over her so fast, three days after our last

visit in the Kilby waiting room. My family had tried to get word to me, but in Kilby they told us our bad news when they felt like it, if at all.

I asked Dane about Pop.

"Better than he was."

They said my father barely came inside the office. If he wasn't sitting in his car in the alley, he was sitting out at Lincoln Cemetery. Dane told me most of his customers were the folks with standing appointments at gravesides, new flowers or cleaning up a stone.

"He's better than he was."

When we were children, we saw our father for a minute at a time on workdays, when he pulled up to get a new fare. A pit stop long enough to find out if we had finished our homework. In summer, he always asked if my luck against the curveball had gotten any better. He would come find us, too, and take his own reports, passing by the ball field or Tullibody High School when classes let out, fathering from the front seat of his car.

My first day home, he pulled up at the end of the taxi line. Pop was still driving his Hudson, and it sounded just as smooth as I remembered. That it had survived, looking as clean as it did when he bought it, meant something. I leaned down on his door, and he dropped his head on the steering wheel.

"Yes, indeed," he said, like he did when Braddock and Schmeling fell, like he did when everything was right with the world. "Yes, indeed."

If tears came, they brought no noise or heaving with them. He stuck his hand out the window and turned up his palm. And I grabbed him. My hands had forgotten the touch of my people, but it had come back in those hours. I held my father's hand tight, rocked it awhile.

"Have you been out there to see your mother?"

"No, sir. Not yet."

"She'll rest better with you home."

"I know she will."

He brought his head off the steering wheel, and looked down the alley and then back and forth. Then he dropped his head once more, this time on my arm. His whiskers and glasses pressed into me. I stood against his taxi, as I had done so many times as a boy, handing him rolls of quarters and dimes and fare slips. My father's hands were leaner than they had once been. We had both aged more than we should have, and the only muscle left was the rugged kind that clung close to the bone. I couldn't tell his pulse from mine, and that was better than anything.

When we got to Lincoln Cemetery, my father backed up to the headstones and parked. Pop got out and opened the trunk, and I followed him. I thought he was getting something out, but no, he had made a seat for us on the edge of the trunk. Though the air was cool and the day-light shorter, the empty trees let that low morning sun get through a little earlier, and it was warm enough to make sitting outside feel all right, or it would have if we were some other place, Riverside or Washington Park, any-where but our family plot.

Some of the grass had faded. Maybe the patch where he always parked grew back slower than the rest. The caretaker had scattered dirt and sand on the bare spots, something for the Saint Augustine runners to grab hold of when the new grass came that spring. Coming down the gravel road we had passed fresh graves, red dirt and slabs, too soon for a stone. When I saw that place and thought of my mother, that raw feeling was all over me again.

Three graves broke the ground in our plot. Aunt Bar-bara and Uncle Walker had passed a few years apart, and they rested under a shared headstone, so my mother wasn't there alone. I had tried to reassure myself with those thoughts, six years of little eulogies every time I thought of her. That was the best I could do, because I couldn't be there. They had me in a field somewhere pull-ing vines on the day they brought her out to Lincoln. I had hoped that she would see me as a free man again. And

I would have been sitting next to her on the porch steps over in Bel-Air instead of sitting near her stone.

I had watched Kilby men die from grieving. They'd swing on a guard or grab hold of the fence. A man would climb as far as he could before the shot came and took him home on a bullet. Those boys just wanted to get back to their people, even if the dead family were the only ones they'd see. I'd thought about doing the same. With the sure-fire guards in the towers, I'd die quickly. What was left of me would have been brought to Lincoln and buried a few steps from where Pop and I sat.

One of his early fares, Mrs. Adair from our church, was still in the cemetery planting bulbs along the fence line. Her husband had been dead for twenty years.

"She didn't worry about you, because she knew you'd be all right when you got home. Said you'd get out a young man still with good years in front of you."

He'd said it too many times for it to be true. She worried to her last day. Had I not done what I did, I would have been home with her. That was dangerous thinking, and she had even warned me about it herself. That first time she visited me, my mother told me that thinking like that was poison. I could tell she'd done her crying before she entered. She was dry-eyed when she spoke.

"You did exactly what you were meant to do. How would you feel if you hadn't? If those men had their way?" she'd said.

"Like the sorriest man in the world."

"You're not that, Nathaniel. We both know."

My mother and father had decided on our names after they read them in a pamphlet from a traveling preacher, Henry McNeal Turner, who had come through Hobson City to start a church. Our folks had a plot in Lincoln Cemetery, and people said Lincoln had freed the slaves, but that preacher talked about a few who had freed themselves, even if they died in the process. Nathaniel Turner. Denmark Vesey. Marie Angelique. They were among the names listed in two columns, like pallbearers carrying their own weight. My people had given us those names, expecting more from us than from the sorry world we were born into. Mama and Pop had been called by their first names all their lives, by adults and children. It galled them to the core. So they said fine. If people were set on calling us by our first names, they would call us by these. Any name-calling might summon something my parents had planted. Everything they gave us, from our names to our work, came from that idea.

"We bought a car," my mother had said. "A taxicab. That new hotel they got going up on the Hill. People need to get there somehow."

Mama announced this as my pop wiped a bit of red dust from the orange paint that made that secondhand ride look a little closer to brand-new. I couldn't have been more than seven, on one of our summer trips to stay with our family in Hobson City. I saw that first taxi when they came to the country to get us, driving the car through all that summer green with paint as bright as something ripe on a vine.

The paint was a shared idea. Mama thought orange would stand out. Pop was partial to houndstooth, like that stingy brim that was never far from his head. And the black cursive lettering. CENTENNIAL HILL TAXI COMPANY, as big as day.

My mother and father met working in a Hobson City carpentry mill. He was fifteen, and in all the working he had done before, that was his first time working for black folks. He made deliveries, on a wagon at first, and then with a truck. The first man to drive it ended up in a ditch, but my father managed to keep the truck on the lopsided roads of Calhoun County without turning it over, so he made decent money hauling pine to the shop and driving pews to the churches. He said that Methodists, Baptists, Garveyites, and Pentecostals all sat on the same grade of lumber that he delivered.

He kept the front seat clear of sawdust and pine tar in case he saw somebody walking along the road, especially the girl from the upholstery shop. He tied the hauling just so, leaving room enough for a few people to hop on the back, and she would always slide over to make room for one more. When my people left Hobson City for Montgomery, they made driving their business, shade-tree jitneys at the start. After they heard that a hotel was in the works on Centennial Hill, Mama and Pop made an enterprise out of what had started as goodwill.

My mother spent most of her time in the stand, but she drove her regulars. When I was inside Kilby, she never drove to visiting day with an empty car. *I couldn't imagine passing somebody on the road without stopping.* I saw her sometimes on my walks across the prison yard back to my cell. She'd make a day of it, circling back and forth with as many as needed a ride.

A couple years before, my father told me that they'd shut down the Hudson assembly line, so he held on to his car for as long as he could. The one we sat in now was not the first, but it had a good fifteen years on it. I heard the age of that car when he rose to his feet, the springs whining underneath us. He took a Thermos and a can of sweet milk from a box in the trunk, and then he picked up two cups, good ones that I recognized from the dining room breakfront.

"Last time I had a decent cup of coffee was with you. We had to grind acorns. Pecans, too," I said.

"Ain't enough sugar to make that go down."

"What sugar?"

"Lord."

After he poured two cups, he pulled spoons from the same box.

"I want you to stop talking about that place."

I nodded, but he wasn't looking at me, just staring straight ahead.

"It's behind you. Been waiting years to say as much, so I'm saying it now. No more reason to speak on it."

"I hear you."

He brought his fist down on my hand and kneaded it.

"Besides, I want to hear about Los Angeles. We can sit down and mark a map before you leave."

"Simple enough. Highway 80 to Route 66," I said.

"That's it?"

"That's it."

"The whole way out?"

"All the way to Los Angeles."

"I've been to Shreveport," he told me. "Past that, I can't do nothing but speculate."

"I haven't seen a thing past Oklahoma."

"You been to Belgium and France and all that."

"That was different."

"No it ain't."

"I mean Los Angeles. I don't know a thing about it. Got to learn my way around is all."

"Boom town. That's all it is. Like all that iron up under Birmingham. Big cities are just country-ass towns that got lucky. You'll learn to drive it like you learned this one. Ain't but two ways to drive. Keep straight or make your corner. I'm either right, or I'm wrong."

"You're right."

"Besides, Nat Cole could throw a rock and hit a man able to drive him. He wants you for that other thing. Ain't no map for that."

Mrs. Adair had moved from the flower beds near the back fence, and made her way to the small cluster of shade trees across the clearing. The last time I had seen her was before the war, and she was elderly then. A line of graves carried her family name, with a handful of empty spaces left.

"I brought Ruby out every day this week. Told me she checked her almanac. First freeze coming next week sometime. I asked what she put down and she say she likes to mix it all up. Let it be a surprise come spring."

She threw a hello in my direction, a garden trowel back and forth above her head. She lifted the garden hat for good measure, showing that gold-and-red scarf wrapped around her hair. I waved right back.

"She told me she put down some of your mother's favorites. Tulips, like the ones she brought into the office a couple times. Of course your mother didn't care for tulips."

"Anemones."

"Yep. Blue ones if she could find them. Course, I told Mrs. Adair tulips were perfect, because your mother would have said likewise."

He hadn't stopped stirring his coffee, though the spoon never touched the cup. He was as careful as always of scratching the bottom or chipping the mouth. My parents didn't get any china when they married, because their relations didn't have much beside well-wishes. The cups my father and I held were what my mother called her marriage china. Paid for in cash, a piece at a time. A new dish every so often when business was good, until they had a full set. Pop's stirring was habit more than thinking, because I could tell his mind had gone off somewhere.

"You know, Pop, they got a Bel-Air out there, too."

"What's that?"

"Bel-Air. Got one in Los Angeles, just like us."

His eyes came back to me then. A smile, too.

"Boy, I saw that Bel-Air in a magazine. Frank Sinatra or somebody. It ain't nothing like ours."

"Nat's got a spread in Hancock Park now. Three-story house."

"Say what?"

"You hear me."

"Three stories. To get that high in Bel-Air, you'd have to climb a tree."

That was the first bit of chuckling I had heard in so long. And the laughing was better than any welcome home I could have heard. Mrs. Adair looked over, and Pop waved that all was well. She gave us one more in kind, rubbing her hands on her skirt first, as though waving how-do called for the cleanest hands. The springs made their noise again when he rose, that time reaching for a second Thermos filled with warm water that he used to rinse both cups and then set them in a box, the dish towel he dried them with folded in between so the porcelain wouldn't chip.

"Believe Mrs. Adair might be ready to get on back. Won't be long. Think you might need to stay for a while."

I nodded.

"I can come back around for you."

"I believe I'll walk on back. Nice as it is."

My father's hand on my shoulder just then felt as big as it used to when I was half his size. Pop was right about me needing some time alone. I sat down in the grass and

looked at my hands. The trembling that had started somewhere in my gut had not made it to the outside yet. And I
wanted to be alone when it did.

As Pop drove away, he circled around on the Lincoln
grass and gave a wide berth to the graves. When he
stopped for Mrs. Adair, he set her box in his trunk while
she shook the dirt from that quilt she'd knelt on. They left
Lincoln slowly, careful of scattering the gravel. Then it
was just me.

I would need that walk when I left Lincoln. It was a good
two miles back to the Hill, almost a straight shot. My legs
were too used to turning at a fence. A straight line from
Lincoln back to the Hill would be the longest walk I had
made with free legs in ten years. Until then I sat on that
grass in front of my mother's stone, my legs outstretched
and my arms out behind me, the way she had seen me so
many times when I sat and listened.

Chapter 9

After I left Lincoln Cemetery, I walked to the garage over on Hall Street. My brother-in-law was under the hood of a Studebaker. Pete stared down, with a shop light close enough to his face to burn him. Marie stood on a ladder inside, hanging fan belts on the empty hooks. Marie had covered her clothes with a smock that matched the coveralls Pete wore. The stitching above the pocket read JEFFRIES AUTOMOTIVE, written in the same green as the Esso sign out front.

"Anybody working today?"

"Be right there," Pete said without looking.

"Ain't got all day," I said.

Then he brought his head from under the hood to see who it was.

"Marie." The first time he said my sister's name, it was a whisper. Then came the shout. "Marie! Baby!"

Pete had my shoulders by then and was shaking me.

He had a good thirty pounds on me, so him grabbing me was something indeed. He shouted for Marie again, but by then she'd come outside and was calling my name. Her voice sounded so sweet, because this time it wasn't choked off from the crying and it wasn't drowning in that Kilby noise. Pete let me go, and my sister's hands were on me then.

"I told you. Wouldn't be long before you got home," she said, something she'd been saying for years. "Told you." She kept saying it, against my shoulder and my cheek and my ear—*told you*—until it was just above a hum that I needed to feel against my ear before it could truly be so.

In most of the baby pictures, Marie was holding me, even if she was just then old enough to carry me on her hip. When I was too big, she settled for punching me dead in my shoulder or thumping me on my forehead. I'd watched her cry too much on our Sundays in the visiting room. On that first day home, the tears were fine, because they were the last she would ever have to cry for me.

She let go of her hug long enough to put both hands on my face.

"You look good."

"Better than I looked yesterday," I told her. "Didn't sleep last night, so ready to get out."

It had barely been a month since the last time she'd seen

me, but on the outside with nothing between her eyes and my face, everything looked different.

"Got something for you out back."

They called it a surprise, but it was a secret that had been talked about for a good long time. We walked through the garage into the backyard, where ten cars lined the fence. My car sat under a cover between a Ford truck and a Mercury. The lines were unmistakably Packard, and the tarp was thin enough to see some of the light flashing on the chrome underneath it.

Pete whipped back the cover, and the wind helped him to bring it free. It was my first time seeing it. The car had been on back order and had arrived two months after I started my sentence. My family painted it the Centennial colors and hired a couple of part-timers to drive. Marie kept the oil changed and the tires good, and always told me the mileage and how much money I had on the books. For ten years it had circled Montgomery without me, racking up 97,000 miles and change. Pete had repainted the checkerboards and the orange with an oyster gray, and the paint carried as much light as the chrome did. Seats in taxis lasted only for so long, so Pete and Marie made decent money in car upholstery. Marie had asked me what I wanted, and I told her charcoal with pinstripes. I wanted the insides to look like a good suit I could wear anytime I had somewhere to go.

"Can't have you headed to Hollywood looking any kind of way. You need to look like you came from somewhere."

"You outdid yourself," I told her. "Both of you."

I leaned into the window to get a better look at the floorboards.

"Redid my mama's house back in April, and we had some extra heartwood."

My Packard came off the assembly line looking like the next one, but the touch of my folks had it looking like no other. I leaned farther into the window until the toes of my shoes were only partly touching the gravel.

"You do know how a car door works. I know you been gone for a while but, damn." Pete opened the door while I was still in the window. "See, just like that."

Dane had given me the money Skip Tate had left, and I took five twenties off the stack and gave them to Pete. He stopped his laughing, and his face changed. He looked like a man with a hundred dollars in his hand.

"Go on, Pete. Fold it up. Put it in your pocket. For the paint and the engine work. I'll send you some more when I get set up."

"You know you don't owe us a dime," Marie said. Pete was quiet, already spending that money in his head.

"Pete, you better fold that and put it in your pocket," I told him.

"Marie's right. You don't owe us a dime." He didn't say it like he meant it.

I peeled off another hundred dollars and put it in Marie's hand. She tried to pull her hand away but I wouldn't let her.

"Here, now. For the seats and for the bookkeeping and the whatnot."

I had been charity for my family for too long. The hours they spent with me were empty ones that they would never get back. I wanted them to have something from me on the books.

"Had my eye on that television at Gray's."

"Every time he walks by, he slows down and stands flat-footed for ten, fifteen minutes."

"They got a sign in the window says you buy a set on your lunch hour, and they'll deliver to your living room by supper time."

Marie held the keys in her hand. Rubbed them with the piece of lamb's wool she'd run along the chrome.

"They give you your license back?"

"I don't need anything else they can give me. Nat's folks got me a California license."

I'd be a bootleg cabbie at best in Montgomery, and whichever cop pulled me over would want my till. If they wanted to pull cabbies over, they waited until a shift was just about done so they could shake somebody down for every dime. Pumping gas and washing windshields was the best I could expect. I saw Johnnie Beechum, the attendant who had worked there years before Marie and Pete bought the place, still cleaning dead things from the windshields, mosquitoes every summer and lovebugs every fall, and I was glad I didn't have to take the offer. I prayed that I'd never have to.

"You want to drive it now, with your California license and all?"

"I'm not through stretching my legs."

When Pete came back out of the garage, his coveralls were off and he had his hat on. The oil was gone from his hands, and he was brushing off the soap flakes that had stuck to his forearm.

"You got a date?" Marie said.

"About to head to Gray's to buy that Zenith," he said, patted the pocket he'd put the money in like she needed proof.

"When you get through, go buy a new hat. Looks like you wore that one in a street fight," I told him.

He took it off and regarded it a bit before he cocked it back on his head. "You know, I just might."

"Not that dime-store mess. Get a Stetson," I said.

"Then I'll get you a new billfold while I'm at it, Nat. Can't carry that kind of money in that dusty wallet you got."

With that he tipped his hat and headed on down the street.

"You don't owe us anything," Marie told me.

"I can do what I want to do again, so I want to do for my folks."

After I followed Marie into the office, a car crossed the bell line and stopped at the gas pump. A black woman was behind the wheel of a DeSoto, wood-sided and full of white children. When she came in, Marie spoke while she took the gas money and counted out the change. The name on her uniform said Lena.

"Let me get a receipt, Marie, because the woman I work for now will swear up and down I took her damn change."

"I got you. Something else, too," Marie told her.

She counted out Lena's change and tapped on a basket of purchase orders. Lena lifted the stack and took a sheet of paper. Some of the kids had gotten out of the car, and one had jumped on the bell line. She looked back to make sure they didn't see her fold that paper into her apron pocket.

"Nosiest children the world has seen. Will run tell any- and everything."

Once she left, Marie lifted the stack and gave me one of the same pages. "Women's Political Council" printed across the top. A newsletter. A list of officers ran down the right-hand side, and my sister's name was near the bottom. Marie Jeffries. Transportation Committee. That's not all she wanted me to see, though.

"I'm only showing you because you asked about her last time."

Though the ink of the machine turned everyone's picture purple and dotted, the face above the column was Mattie. Letter from the Editor. And the signature, the first name familiar, and her married name. Matilda Allen.

Marie looked over my shoulder to see what I was reading. And she left her chin right there, and that bit of sighing she did came down on my collarbone.

"You got a whole new life coming to you. So you don't have to dwell."

"How is she?"

"She's fine." Paused too long. So much she could have said then.

Yes, my years had been long, but they had been just as empty. I had gathered no memories strong enough to quiet the old notions.

"Like I said. A whole new life."

Marie and Mattie had gotten close when we dated. We had gone to see *Murder in Harlem* with Marie and Pete at the State Theater. *I like that girl, Nathaniel. You and me, both,* I'd told her. My sister helped me pick the ring, and she was the one who sold it for me, and used that money to pay off the note on the Packard.

"Would it be better if she'd waited for you?"

I shook my head. I saw the women who had waited on Kilby men. Young women. Old women. I'd watched enough of the regulars age in the visiting room, getting years-deep in the waiting.

"You'll have somebody soon."

Marie straightened up the newsletters and hid them beneath the purchase orders. She had told me to move on. And I surely would. But I needed to see Mattie's face, and hear her voice, if only to say good-bye. That was as close to the good times as I could ever be again. Friend was not enough, but it was all I could have. But before I could see a friend, I needed a stranger.

Chapter 10

Mama Nonie's Grill sold coffee and doughnuts in the front vestibule, and a small luncheonette served sandwiches and hot plates in the main room. A long row of high-back booths stretched beyond the pony wall. The girls would come around and talk to you, see what was on your mind. And if you had come looking for something in particular, they would show you to the back stairs that led to the cathouse floor.

The young lady who sat next to me said her name was Sue. And I told her my real name, because if I was ashamed I wouldn't have been there. We made plans, me and Sue. We talked about how long and how much money and it all sounded good to me. She drank straight bourbon out of a julep cup.

"What you drinking, friend?"

"Some whiskey I can't even pronounce," I told her.

"Guess you can call it what you want, then."

I had ordered the oldest whiskey they had, ten years old, some that got bottled up around the same time I did. I could pretend that my time did to me what it had done to that liquor.

"Take your time," she told me.

"Make sure you do the same when we get upstairs."

They charged by the hour, and she told me I could get a second go around if I still had my wind. And I told her I'd see when we got upstairs, because I wasn't thinking about a clock. And when she rubbed her hand up my arm and back down again, it took everything I had to keep my head straight. I took my hand off my glass then, because I didn't want my neat shot of liquor to tremble and spill all over. I had never been a clumsy man around women, in either conversation or in close quarters, and I didn't want to start then. I had been itching for so long. Every part of me was knotted up, and I needed to get right.

"First time lounging over here, or you know how it works?"

"Both," I told her. "Yes and yes."

I pointed to her glass.

"Fine right now, but after a while. Bartender will send a setup to the room. I like me a slow-drinking bourbon in the afternoon. A little something to make it sweet. And you, some of that old long-name whiskey."

She touched me again, just a tip of her nail on the back

of my hand. A circle on my skin. For so long the touch had been my own, grabbing myself by the handful, and letting every rub and push and pull take me from this world to one that was better, where the women who crossed my mind stayed until the walls shook and crumbled, and then I was alone and emptied out. In the end the best of my conjuring would be just another stain on my jailhouse mattress.

"Thank you for the drink, friend," she told me. "Third floor. Last door on the right."

The upstairs light came through the lead glass and transoms. Cloudy glass let in the sun but still hid the business. I needed that light as much as I needed that grind. I wanted to get to Mama Nonie's in the daylight, because I needed to see every bit of the woman in that room with me. Sue and me there butt-naked with sunshine on us. Every time she said something to me I told her to say it again. True or not didn't matter to me, but every word came floating right along with her bourbon and sweet to-bacco still on her tongue, and it stuck to me just like that bedsheet cotton did once it lost its grip on the mattress. The sheets let loose like I did until I was too weak to move. And then we were still for a while. Sunlight and the breeze came through the same window and ran up my leg, and touched me where she had. I was wet and cool and warm all at once.

Sue walked to the chest of drawers and fixed two drinks

from that setup tray. Bourbon and whiskey, a saucer of limes, a bowl of ice, and a jelly glass with sugar cubes. She spooned two ice cubes and poured the liquor over.

"You were in Kilby," she said.

It wasn't a question. I didn't say anything right off, but she waited and watched me.

"Got out this morning," I said.

"You smell like that soap. That don't mean you smell bad or anything, just familiar."

She drained into my glass some of the cool water at the bottom of the ice bowl, and then she poured a couple of fingers of whiskey.

"They sent me to the girls' home for a while. I made soap in the industrial school," she said. Crushing cubes in her teeth, the first sugar and the second ice.

"That lye would splash sometimes when we poured the buttermilk. Worse than grease burns. They made us wear those long leather gloves. Came up to here," she said, drawing a line on her arm just above her elbow.

While we did our business, she never let herself roll too far from that nightstand. That top drawer was where she kept whatever she had for men set on trouble. She took a long sip of her cool drink, then another, the whole time quiet and looking, considering me.

"Figured it was Kilby. Boys go to Atmore and come out too old for this here."

The knock on the door was light, but enough to remind me of the time. The college tower was close enough to hear the quarter tolls, so my second hour had come and gone. She set her drink on the night table.

"You squared away, friend?"

"I believe so."

"All right, then," she said. "Fresh towels in the closet."

She nodded toward the bathroom.

"Don't worry, we got store-bought soap."

They charged an extra dime to use the shower, and a customer dropped his money in the can next to the Dixie Cups and Listerine. When the hot water filled the bowl, that ammonia cream on the porcelain burned my nostrils. The towels from the linen closet smelled like bleach. I didn't mind, because if I ever held a Kilby towel to my nose, I was liable to smell the last man's funk, so the cathouse bleach, heavy enough to water my eyes, was welcome. Once the last of the prison soap was gone, I walked out of Mama Nonie's cleaner than that Kilby water had ever gotten me.

Marie had told me where I could find Mattie, and I was in decent shape to see her then. The Women's Political Council had no standing office. Organizing made some folks nervous, and they'd been called communists and the like. They worked from places that were hidden and temporary. For most of November, they had worked out of the needlework shop above Pearletta's Cleaners. Marie said that Mattie still taught two or three English classes at the college, and in the afternoons, she worked on the newsletter that most weeks had a headline about the women thrown off the busses. If I wanted to find her, that's where she'd be. Marie wasn't sure if it was a good idea, but of course, neither was I. Just something that had to be done.

The door next to Pearletta's opened to a flight of stairs. The sign above the railing said ALTERATIONS with an arrow pointing the way. I stopped near the top, and I looked through the railings and the picture windows that lined the wall. The room was as wide as the two storefronts downstairs, and the ceiling was high enough for two rows of clothes on the walls. Each work stall had a wardrobe rack and a sewing machine, some old and foot-powered and others electric. The downtown seamstresses from Loveman's and Montgomery Fair made their side money on Union Street. The place had not changed since the times I'd gone there as a boy, dropping off our school uniforms.

The machines were still, and the evening work waited on the racks. Hours on the door said 5:30 p.m. to 9:00 p.m. or by appointment. It was just after four o'clock. The only seamstress working, red-and-white measuring tape draped around her neck, leaned over a cutting table folding papers instead of fabric. She worked in front of a row of curtains that cut the room in two.

She turned and spoke to someone on the other side, Mattie. I got a quick glance before the seamstress turned the curtain loose. I could have let seeing her be enough and turned around, but I didn't. I walked up to the door, and the seamstress saw me before I knocked. Her look was pleasant and cautious. She folded a corner of fabric over her work before she walked to the door.

"Hello, ma'am. Nathaniel Weary, and I'm looking for— Mrs. Allen. Matilda Allen."

"Oh, you're Marie's brother. She and Pete are friends of mine," she said, extending her hand. "Louise McCauley. My husband cuts your nephew's hair."

The room had been quiet, but motors started turning behind the curtain. One, then a second and a third revved with enough power to blink the lights. It was too strong for sewing machines, and a clockwork rumbling filled the place with a hum.

Mrs. McCauley was behind the curtain for some time, longer than it should take to give a name. The sound wouldn't let me listen to what was being said, but then the spinning slowed, and each machine went quiet. I would have liked the noise to stay with us.

"Mr. Weary, come on back," she said. "Oh, and welcome. Welcome back home."

I was already holding my hat, so I dipped my head instead. I moved back the curtain to see Mattie clutching her arms. It felt like everything in me tightened until it froze, except for my heart and my breathing, too fast to do me any good.

"All this time." She unfolded her arms and hugged me close, a touch that used to mean the world to me. "Prayed for you every day."

If anyone had walked through the door it would have looked exactly like it was, me and her holding on too long and too tight. But that was all that was left for us. That little bit of time.

"Marie told me I could find you here," I said, stepping away then. Looking around. "Hasn't changed much has it?"

"No. I'm still bringing our Easter clothes and school uniforms. My children."

"How old?"

"Five. Twins. Clara and Reginald."

"That's good, Mattie."

That was the best I could say.

"I'm here more than I'm home. Marie told you about the busses?"

"Heard it got worse."

"We've been saying we're going to do something for the longest. Here we are."

She had found herself a good fight at least. That time

she would have spent fighting for me, if only in her heart and her thinking, might have taken everything. Maybe she'd have been too spent to think twice about a bus or a life anything close to whole. We both might have been too thankful for the half measures the world had given us.

"You did something," she told me. "I watched you do what nobody should ever have to."

"Look where it got me."

"Look where it got Nat Cole. Alive. Those men didn't think anybody would get there in time. They thought they could do what they wanted and when. They can't think like that forever. Got to end sometime."

She studied my face while I did hers, taking in the changes all at once.

"There's something else," she said, reaching for the bag on a chair in the corner. "I knew your day was coming soon, and I've been carrying this. I was meaning to take this to Marie to give to you. In case I didn't get a chance."

She opened an envelope and pulled out the photograph that I had never seen, me and the Nat Cole Trio in the Empire's dressing room. The look on my face those years ago made me feel like a stranger. Cocksure and smiling, as I should have been in that army uniform, smiling because Mattie had told me to.

"Marie told me about your job, and I wanted you to have it before you left."

As much good as it did me to see it, I wondered about the other pictures. The ones with me and her together. Asking about them would have sounded ungrateful in the face of her kindness.

Someone knocked on the door, then two hands, small ones, knocking at once. Then came Mrs. McCauley's steps as she opened it, setting the door chimes to ringing. Mattie pulled back the curtains as her children came through the door. They had on the Saint John plaid that some of the schoolchildren wore walking back and forth on Union Street.

"Clara. Reginald. This is my friend, Mr. Weary," she said.

They introduced themselves, but the whole time distracted by the picture I held. The unmistakable face of Nat King Cole.

"I know who that is," the boy said.

"Me, too," I told them.

"Me, three. He's on the radio," said Clara.

She told her mother about her day, good news first. A gold star in spelling and a torn hem on the swing set. Mrs. McCauley, across the room with a pincushion and thread, called the girl over. Clara stood on a Nehi crate as the hem was repaired. She had been singing and twirling about, but when Mrs. McCauley took to the hem, she stood still. Whatever song she had started continued a little softer as she mouthed it and worked her fingers, playing the tune in her head. Mattie's son marked his place in an Alice and Jerry book with a baseball card. Roy Campanella. When he started reading, he put that bookmark through the spokes of the Singer and worked the foot pedal, filling the place with the tap of that metal on the card.

"Thank you," I told her, speaking low. That was the appropriate thing to let her hear. The rest of the old feelings weren't dead yet, but I didn't want to stir them. Maybe the moving and the working and the new life would clear it all out.

"It's all in front of you now."

This was the Montgomery I had returned to. A young girl had been thrown off a bus, handled like she was a grown man and not a child. Mattie Green Allen couldn't let that go. And it did me well knowing. We were joined in something at least, in what we thought about the city. We both needed to be some other place. Mine I'd find by leaving, and hers she'd make by changing things at home. Making that new place together was a bygone notion. I had to be fine with that.

I made my way out of the door, and Mattie set her machines to spinning once more. They had heated up enough that I could smell the oil and the ink, something like kerosene, a smell that stayed with me until I got outside. When I got to the street, I stood on the corner with

the late-afternoon riders waiting for the City Lines. Some
held transfers and the others dimes. A couple stretched
and leaned, trying to get a better view down the street.
You expect a certain posture from people when work is
over. But no. Where people might have been at ease, they
got rigid, as though more work waited. One man had his
hat clutched already, revealing a head full of hair, every bit
of it gray. A nervous smile crossed his face. Maybe he was
ready to throw some kindness in the driver's face and pray
that man was feeling too good or was too tired for mess.

In the copy of Mattie's newsletter I'd taken, the right
column listed names of harassed and assaulted bus riders.
Claudette Colvin. Geneva Johnson. Viola White. Katie
Wingfield. Epsie Worthy. Mary Louise Smith. Hilliard
Brooks. The police shot and killed him when he wouldn't
get off. The stories were followed by a question. "Do we
want these to end up like Emmett Till?" I rolled the newsletter in my hands as a woman passed me on the way to
the stop.

"You didn't see the bus coming?"

"No ma'am. Can't say I did."

"Thanks all the same."

"Ma'am," I told her, "something to read along with your
paper."

I showed her the newsletter.

"Thank you, sweetheart, but that's all right." She told

me this as she pulled from her pocketbook a copy of the same. She slipped it back in and retrieved her fare from an inside pocket. From the sound of the rattling, she had enough change at the ready and wouldn't have to search while the driver waited. They gave people hell for that.

"And don't look so sad," she told me, and smiled enough for the both of us.

Then I saw it coming over her shoulder. It shifted gears to take the hill, and the noise announced it to anyone who had not yet seen. She heard it but didn't turn around. Her face went blank, and she was ready to get on. After she climbed the steps, she dropped her fare. The driver didn't wait for her to find a place to sit. She was still walking to the back as the bus rolled away.

Chapter 11

I had already packed the car for California, so my trunk dipped as Dane and I sat parked on High Street. Dane had ridden with me up Highway 31 and back, while I burned the carbon off my engine. We took it up some of the back roads in pine country, about half a tank's worth of driving, and then we came on back to town. Evening settled in outside my window, and brought with it my last Saturday night in Montgomery.

We parked across from the State Theater, where a group stood, teenagers and college kids, deciding which of the movies to see. One side of the marquee said *Blackboard Jungle*, and the other listed a James Dean double feature. *Rebel Without a Cause* and *East of Eden* ran back-to-back. When I'd gone the day before, the girl making popcorn had told me why. He had died two months before. I wish I hadn't known, because I thought about it the whole time I watched him fighting on a mountainside. I didn't stay for the second show.

The third screening room wasn't listed on the marquee, and Dane told me why. A coalition too new to have a name had rented it out to discuss the busses. They talked about staying off for a day and asking for Negro seating that was first-come, first-serve, from the back to the front. Some wanted more, and some wanted nothing. Folks had been gathering separately all over the city. Professors. Taxi drivers. Voters League. Women's Council. And for the first time they would be in one place at one time to talk about what to do next. They did not want to attract the attention of the police or informants, so they hid their meeting in the middle of Saturday night, on a strip of town where it was easy to blend in.

The taxi drivers had learned the hard way. When I was young, they had tried to organize to get Negro drivers in the taxi line at Union Station. They had meetings, too many and too public, and before long the taxi commission and the police got wind of it. Any number of things could make a driver think twice. Sugar in the gas tanks, broken windows, and slashed tires were the kinds of things done in the dark. The rest the police did in broad daylight without the slightest hesitation. A handful of parking tickets left a driver owing the city more than he made. That was enough to make most think twice about changing things.

With the busses, they had learned to be more careful. No more meetings in schools or homes. It was better if a meeting looked like a party or a funeral or a picture show, where cabs lined up on a side street was to be expected.

Dane had been elected sergeant at arms for the Taxi Guild. In the early days, he was just in charge of bringing the folding tables and coffee cups. But the job had changed as the times required. He still showed up at every meeting, but he sat outside in his cab. He watched who was going into the State Theater, and he looked out for anybody cruising and paying too much attention to cars and license plate numbers.

"There," Dane said, nodding. "Blue Ford. Sam Collins. Can't say he's the last one I'd suspect, but, you just don't know 'til you know."

ALLIED TAXI was hand-painted on the side of his car. Sam had driven by slowly once before, but he wasn't looking for fares. A couple coming out of Hilltoppers Barbeque had their hands raised, and the man even whistled. Sam Collins didn't even see or hear them, because by then he was off the brake and heading back around the corner.

I remembered him. He had worked for Centennial off and on, but he'd worked for pretty much anybody who'd let him pick up a shift or two. He couldn't hold his liquor any better than he could hold a dollar. Dane heard he'd had a couple of misdemeanors, and he'd done a little time in county jail. I had done time with men just like him. If the only thing between getting out and dropping some years was to give the police a name, then they'd tell everything.

He came back around and stopped right next to us. He stared right in my face, and then he saw Dane.

"All right now, Sam."

"Hey there, Dane. Heard some of the guild folks called a meeting over this way."

"Yeah. You know Rita Tucker? Owns a little hot dog stand down on Catoma?"

He nodded, kind of.

"Wants to make a little parking lot and a cabstand on her property. Getting her paperwork together for the zoning board. She asked the guild to come down and speak at the hearing."

"Oh."

"Be nice, won't it? Shed and a picnic table. Pay phone. Won't have to worry 'bout parking tickets on your windshield down at Union Station."

"Didn't know a thing about it. Heard some of the boys say they were headed over here."

"I just got called this morning. Rita just got word from zoning yesterday. They meet Monday. All kind of paperwork."

He nodded, and then he looked at me for a good little while.

"Been a while, Nathaniel."

"While and a half, Sam. Good to see you."

"How long you been home?"

"Couple-three days."

"I know you happy to be out from 'round there."

"Yes, indeed."

"I know the feeling."

There was something in Sam's face that I didn't want to read, so I looked away. Maybe he was working the only hustle he had. Tell his handlers old news too stale to hurt anybody. Maybe he loved the way it made him feel to tell something. Maybe it was just money.

His Ford idled too hard. Most folk who made a living driving a car wouldn't let it ride that bad. He kept looking back toward the theater. A couple of drivers from Metropolitan and Carver Park walked inside. While Sam looked away, an old woman walked out of the tobacco store with a carton of Old Golds under her arm.

"Evening," she said. Looked at us and said it again.

Sam didn't pay attention to the woman until she opened the door and was halfway in the backseat.

"Evening, ma'am."

"You working?"

Seems like he had to think about it. "Yes, ma'am."

"Washington Park, please. Roosevelt and Hill."

He looked at us, and was still glancing toward the theater.

"Go ahead and make your money, Sam," Dane told him. "Stop by the stand Monday, we'll have some minutes typed up for you and the boys who couldn't make the meeting."

And with a last look and a so long, he was off.

"What happens when he finds out you lied to him?"

"No lie. If he carries his ass to the zoning meeting, he'll see Rita Parker waiting for a hearing. If he's telling on us, whatever he says has to be right. Not all the time, but enough. Else they'll find another one we don't know about."

With Sam Collins gone, Dane could relax. He had been sitting up looking stiff and a little nervous, too tense to sink deep into his seat. He leaned back on the headrest and took in some of Saturday night. Thanksgiving was coming, and the cool weather had brought out the heavy coats. The football team had a game that afternoon, and college kids had come from campus in black-and-gold sweaters. Some stood in front of the movie house, and others gathered at Hilltoppers, waiting to get a bite to eat before curfew came and the dorm mothers locked the doors.

"Hope you plan to say good-bye before you leave," Dane told me. "I know you lied and said Monday, but this trunk is too heavy."

"I figured I'd say good-bye tonight without you knowing. Hugging and crying ain't the way to start a trip. Plus Eleanor might try to feed me before I go in the morning.

Have me nodding off to sleep and in a ditch somewhere in Mississippi."

I tried to make light of it, but I couldn't say a proper good-bye to family I hardly knew. I had been a stranger to my brother's children. I had heard family stories that were new to me. So many times over those days, my loved ones told stories that started with remember when. And for me, the answer was a silent no, but I listened, hearing things that were unfamiliar, painfully so. Every story fell into the hole left by the things I'd missed.

"It'll be good for you out there," Dane said. "You'll see some things. Might see Nancy Wilson."

"If I do, I'll tell her Dane said hello."

"Autographs. The kids say they want some. Doesn't matter who, just anybody famous."

"I'll send as many as I can. Pictures, too."

Around the time the meeting let out, a delivery truck pulled up and left a bundle of evening papers in the box outside Parker's Pharmacy. Dane got out and bought one. While he stood there, reading and flipping, a young man spoke to him. I'd seen him leave the bus meeting a while before. He was dressed like a professor in that tweed the teachers wore, but the clergy pin gave him away. He had a paper bag in one arm, and in the other, a topcoat and a briefcase with corner marks in the leather from a multitude of books.

I could tell what they were saying without hearing a word. My brother pointed to the car, offering a ride, and the preacher pointed toward the corner, saying he was fine walking. Dane shook his head and took the paper bag and the young man followed. I leaned back and popped the door before Dane had to reach for it.

"Martin, my brother Nathaniel. Nat, this is Reverend King. The new Improvement Association—the folks meeting across the street. Rev's running it."

"It's running me, I believe."

I turned to shake his hand. As young as he was, he looked just as tired. Saturdays could be hard on a preacher. Weddings and funerals, maybe both in a day. On top of that, figuring what to say the next morning. The day had caught up with him. New stubble covered his face along with the razor bumps that hadn't healed all the way.

"Welcome home," he said, nodding into his hello. "I saw your picture on the wall in Malden's. I saw you standing next to Nat Cole and thought you were a musician. Then somebody told the story. One said it was a trombone and the other said trumpet."

"In actuality, Rev, it was a microphone."

He settled back in his seat. "A microphone."

He wore the clothes that concealed a day's worth of rumpling. Tie and a vest, that same sturdy wool, so the top layers of his clothes could keep him looking fresh long after he was spent.

"They tell me Nat Cole's father used to preach here."

"Over at First Baptist, matter of fact," I told him.

"Reverend Abernathy's place," he said.

"Nat played piano fifth Sundays with the children's choir," I told him. "Couldn't have been more than six years old. Had as many people showing up for him as they had for communion."

"I get on that upright every now and again, but I could never play like that. Good to calm the nerves," Martin said.

He was quiet for a minute, and then he pulled himself toward us with both hands, his arms resting on the back of our seat.

"I need to ask you all something. I couldn't ask any of the preachers or association folks. They might think I'm— well, unappreciative. Why do you think they chose me for this? All the people to put in charge, and they chose me."

We'd reached his house by then, and Dane pulled to the curb before he answered.

"From what I heard, everybody thinks you're smart. The white reporters love to quote some ignorant preacher. You ain't that. That's the first thing. Second, you're from Atlanta. And I got to be honest, Rev. If the white folks run you out of town, you'll have somewhere better to go."

"Not a thing wrong with honesty. Better to hear it to my face, I imagine."

I heard him gathering up his things then, and that satchel had some weight to it, too much to be carrying around all day. As much as folks talked about walking, they would have to learn to travel light.

"Been in a few Packards, but I've never seen a pinstripe seat," he said.

"This is Nathaniel's car. He always wanted a hat like this, but with a skull as large as his, it wasn't feasible. Mama said if she bought that much fabric, she could just reupholster a car instead. He could roll his head around the headrest and the seat and be satisfied."

The young preacher looked at us like we were crazy, but that good kind of crazy that he preached about. Fiery furnaces and lion's dens and that kind of crazy.

"No shame in a big head. The sign of a thinking man," he said.

The porch light came on and his wife peeked through the curtain while she cradled a baby. All I could see of the child was an arm, a small hand around the mother's thumb. The curtain moved like Mrs. King did, back and forth to keep the baby calm.

"How old?"

"Three weeks."

"Your first?" I could feel him smiling before I saw as much in the rearview. Smiling and saying yes.

"The young girl who was put off the bus back in March, the Colvin girl, you all know her?"

"Know some of her people," I told him. "Good folk."

"I guess you don't have to know her for it to be a shame." He looked toward the house. "Well, next time. I figure we'll be ready."

It was a neat little place, and it had been the parsonage for as long as I had been alive. The preachers had all been old before, so his was the first young family. The first baby born in that house.

"Porch looks good," Dane told him.

"Had some paint left from the nursery. I thought the swing might be good for Yoki. They tell me it might not be a good idea, sitting on my front porch. Things might get ugly."

"It's been ugly for a while, Rev."

Dexter Avenue Baptist Church was half a block from the State Capitol, but the parsonage was a mile away, on the last block of Centennial Hill. The distance made that house feel more like a home, no different than the ones of the doctors and professors who lived in the houses next door. It was quieter that I would have expected, even with Saint Margaret's emergency room across the street.

I looked back at the preacher, and I thought at first he was looking at his family. His house. But that tiredness had made its way to his eyes, and he was sound asleep just that fast.

"Martin? Rev?"

When he came to, he said something with a nervous chuckle, a bit embarrassed. "I appreciate the ride."

"Ain't a problem. And remember what I said. Once the mayor sees we got the right man in charge, you'll have the bus thing figured out in a week or two."

His nod was gracious if not certain.

"Good luck to you in California," he told me.

"Good luck to you here," I told him.

With his door open, he paused for a minute, and said the rest of it.

"I saw Nat Cole in Boston. Storyville. Shook his hand. He wouldn't know me from Adam, but let him know he has friends in Montgomery."

"I'll be sure to pass that along, Rev."

He waved his thank-you to us once his wife opened the door, and then it closed behind them. Once they were in for the evening, the twin porch light fixtures went dark.

"How old do you think he is?"

"They said he's twenty-five. Maybe a little older, but young."

"God bless him," I said. "Y'all need to tell him to be careful walking around at night. Especially with his name in the paper."

"Why you think I gave him a ride?"

"Over in a couple of weeks," I said. "That's what you told him."

"I had to tell him something. Felt bad after I told him he might get run out of town, as true as it is. I had to leave him on a good note, at least. It's not your worry anyhow. You got to get up early and leave without saying good-bye. Just don't forget my pictures. Nancy Wilson. Sarah Vaughan. Dorothy Dandridge."

He went on like that half the way home, turning the radio dial and calling that sweetheart roll.

Chapter 12

I lined up my nickels along the top of the pay phone across from the gas station. I didn't know how much change me and Nat Cole would talk through. Beechum was the only one pumping gas on Sundays. He lived next door in the duplex, where he ran a fix-it shop out of the first floor. He dealt with typewriters, lawn mowers, sewing machines, mainly. Anything with a spring or a motor. He wore coveralls and black Stacy Adams shoes, and he sat in a chair under a tree that marked the property line.

Skip Tate gave me Nat's phone number along with a package of things I needed to look over before I made my way west. While Beech filled up the Packard and the two gas cans I left by the pump, I got on the phone. The voice of the operator was Sunday-morning sweet.

"How may I direct your call?"

"Los Angeles," I said. "York 54981."

After her thank-you, three rings and then an answer.

"Hello?"

I was ready for someone else, but Nat answered.

"Hello, Nat? It's Weary."

"Good old Nat Weary," he said. "Happy to know you're back home."

"Sorry to call so early—"

"Not at all. Been up for a while. This thing in my head, I needed to hear how it sounds."

The music behind him was low, and I only heard it when he was silent. Trying to hear that song, I was quiet for a little too long.

"Weary? You there?"

"Just wanted to call and let you know I'm about to hit the road."

"Good. There's a room for you at the Dunbar. Elizabeth and Walter work for us, and they rent out a couple of houses around Avalon. Said they have a place opening up that you're welcome to. First of December."

"I'm sure it'll be fine. Better than fine. Want you to know I appreciate all this."

"We'll be lucky to have you."

"But—"

Didn't quite know how to say it.

"You don't owe me this, you know. That man got what he had coming."

"But you. What'd you get?"

Again the words didn't come right off. It was easier to listen. I had missed years of his music, so much of it was new and classic at the same time.

"What's the name of the song?"

"That's the hardest part sometimes," he said. "Maybe by the time you get here I'll have one for it. Safe traveling."

I held the phone awhile after he was gone. I started to collect my unused nickels, but I decided to leave them. A little bit of fortune for whoever came next.

Chapter 13

I stood in Nat's light, and I saw how that NBC stage would look to him once the first episode began. Beneath all that heat, a man couldn't do anything but sweat. While Nat sat in his dressing room, the director asked me to stand in his place onstage. Bob Henry needed to get the lights just so, and he needed someone close to Nat's color and his height to stand where he would and move through his marks from center stage to the piano. Instead of a spotlight, the television studio had lamps on a grid overhead, shining down at all kinds of angles. Some hit me directly, and others lit the spots I walked to, following the same steps that Nat would take that evening.

The camera and the microphone, both on wheels with brakes and handles, trailed me and stopped just over my shoulder as I sat at the Steinway's bench. I had followed the tape on the cement floor, hitting every mark. When Bob asked me to turn my head and look at the camera, I did so. Staring at the three lenses, and not knowing which was the right one, I just looked at the chrome carriage bolt in the center of them, and I ignored that microphone that dropped down, close enough for me to reach.

"We need a level. Say a little something for us, Weary."

Bob leaned around that camera when he said as much, looking at me with the headphones pressed a little tighter to his ears. I had an audience of workers, a skeleton crew of apprentices setting up chairs for the orchestra. One wheeled in a cart of kinescopes. The fellow unrolling sound cable looked up for a minute, like what I was about to say meant something.

"Give me a second, and I'll think of something clever."

Someone behind the rack of monitors raised a thumb. I couldn't tell whose it was, but that thumb gave way to wiggled fingers.

"Need a read on the keys, Weary."

I'd be a fool to pretend like I knew what I was doing, but I remembered a little from the few music lessons I'd had. So I played for the NBC people a familiar sound, G-E-C, the three keys of that peacock's call. I got a smile or two, and a little bit of that nervous laughing people did. The whole lot of them were anxious.

Half of the sales department came in and out, and Nat told me to never miss a chance to eavesdrop, because any news, good or bad, would come from them. I heard the secretaries saying the salesmen had calls out to would-be sponsors, telling them to watch. Hearing about it wasn't enough, but seeing it that evening would be enough to bring it home for Nat. A nervous-looking salesman was a sorry sight, and I hoped they'd have enough sense to stand a little farther from the camera line or else put a good face on.

Walking the studio halls at NBC and passing other sets, I saw how far money could take somebody. That Texaco coin bought a top-notch backdrop, a blue-skied city with a filling station on every corner. In front of that canvas, they would roll out those shiny gas pumps, real ones, with a Texaco star made of red and white glass. That Buick money had bought Milton Berle a marquee, and Chevrolet had put plenty of sparkle on that sign of Dinah Shore's. Burbank was too young a town for a full-grown skyline, so the closest thing to a cityscape hung from the rafters.

Nat's backdrop was simple but it did what it needed to. The black canvas had holes punched out of the line-drawn buildings, and the bulbs shining through the openings looked like bright windows on a clear city evening. Nat would sing from the valley of a make-believe Los Angeles, and the night sky would glow with gaslight crowns flickering behind him. With no sponsor and his own money, he built his city any way he could, and it looked decent enough considering.

I had watched the shop apprentice jigsaw a piece of balsa wood, taking it from a sheet to a crown that Friday during rehearsal. It gave me something to do while Nat sat in a meeting that was an hour longer than the run-through. Mackie had been an apprentice for his father, who had worked at NBC since the radio days. Apprentices were all that Nat's show could afford, but Mackie was one of those who jumped at it. A hit show would turn an apprentice into a full-timer that much faster, and put some money in his pocket at the same time. Mackie covered the crown in black shellac and painted the letters a pearly gloss, until that balsa had a candy apple shine.

"You showed me something with that crown," I told him.

"Longboards. I made a couple, and my old man figured I might be a carpenter after all. Mr. Cole ought to do a beach episode. Surfers. The whole nine."

"He finds somebody to pay the bills, and he just might."

Mackie made a stand for the sign and covered the spindle in axle grease so the spinning would be as smooth as the finish. Once he'd screwed it on the post, he set it in a bucket of concrete. That would be Nat's logo and signature until some sponsor put a name above his. Mackie gave it a whirl, and that crown spun like it would never stop turning.

So Nat King Cole had a crown at least. He paid for it himself, but it was still a crown. When I walked past Mackie's shop stall that day of the first show, he was still cleaning. The racket he was making that time was not the jigsaw but the vacuum, clearing a day's worth of dust that had dulled the fixtures. I waited for the noise to die before I told him what I had for him, one of the 45s Nat wanted me to hold and pass to the shop boys.

"A little something from Mr. Cole. Let you know we appreciate you."

His tools were still ringing in his ears, so his thank-you sounded like a shout, but sincere all the same. He sliced through the seal with a pocketknife, and he wiped his hands before he touched the record, careful of getting dust on the vinyl.

"Won't be in stores until the New Year most likely, so you and the boys will be the first."

Mackie took a little look at his record, one side and the other, before he returned it to the sleeve, the grooves shining like that handmade crown.

"Say, Weary, some of the guys are getting chairs from the prop house. I'll save one for you."

"I appreciate it, but I got a spot by the board where I can see everything. You boys stretch out and enjoy it."

With that he was gone, off to claim his seat in those last minutes before the show. Of course, they didn't need seats really, because the show was all of fifteen minutes.

Thirteen and a half minutes of singing and a little touch of small talk, because NBC wanted to give the people as much Nat Cole as they could in that time. The handwriting on the cue cards matched the rundown on the chalkboard. Even the banter was timed, never more than thirty seconds' worth at a stretch.

The only choreography was a cool walk from one mark to the next until Nat sat down at the bench, where he would let his fingers steal the show. He wanted anybody watching to see it up close. Mackie had done what Nat had asked for and prepped that Steinway for a star turn. He'd added a strip of mirror along the case so that the keys, their reflections, and a double of set of hands would fill the frame. So with that piano and a spinning wooden crown, Nat Cole was half an hour from showtime.

My personal history with television had been brief. I had cut my teeth with the soundie box at the pool hall on Thurman Street. It was a jukebox with a little movie to go with the song. We'd watch the bands clown and smile at the front row girls who smiled and winked right back, showing all that leg. We'd go in together, Dane and our friends, pooling our money to make a nickel. My mother said those machines were indecent, a frog's hair away from being a peep show. That was the whole point of it, standing back there in the darkest corner where the tube light shined brightest. That box disappointed as much as it thrilled, because the soundie machine was liable to cut off before the song was over, slice the picture in two, or blink so much that the picture was more kaleidoscope than anything else.

Our first real television experience wasn't much better. On colored night at the Alabama State Fair, half of the carnies had the night off, so the television in the Future World booth wasn't even on. With no picture and no power, the television was only a piece of furniture, half wood and half glass. The line moved quickly with nothing there to see. The world seemed better off with our radios and speculation.

Television had always been a small thing. I could find a better picture at the movie house, and the music sounded better on a 45 or the radio. Watching music on a small screen had been a young idea before I went away. Ten years later every house I'd been in had chairs gathered around a television like they once did fireplaces. And on that first evening of *The Nat King Cole Show*, I couldn't imagine any seat empty. Showtime was close, so the viewers were surely gathering to see him just as I walked toward the dressing room.

NBC covered the walls with posters of the stars. Milton Berle and Steve Allen. Next to him, the host of *General Electric Theater*, Ronald Reagan. A framed picture of Nat hung between Steve Allen and Loretta Young, just outside his dressing room. Beneath the star his placard filled the slot, his name spelled out in those thick, glossy letters.

The lights continued to make me sweat. When I opened his dressing room door, he saw a few beads still on my forehead and the bit that darkened my shirt. He handed me a cloth from the stack on the makeup table.

"Lights are something else, aren't they?"

"Like that kind they put on a brisket," I told him. "I did your sweating for you, so you'll be fine."

After Nat lit a cigarette, he almost put the lighter in his jacket pocket, then remembered, and placed it on the counter. The shape of anything in his pocket would show on camera and the lights would pick up a bad line. His suit was shinier than the ones he usually wore, and his lapels caught a little more of the light. That way the cut of his shoulder wouldn't get lost against the backdrop. He wrapped his pocket square around a piece of cardboard, because they couldn't have it falling in the middle of a song. Nothing could be out of place in front of a live camera.

Nat was on edge. He didn't look nervous, but he didn't quite know what to do with his hands, and the fingers gave him away, shuffling something nobody could see.

"Tell me something, Weary."

"Tell you what?"

He shrugged. "Anything at all. Just tell me something."

I stole a mirror glance, making sure I looked as relaxed

as we both were supposed to be. Skip talked about this part of things, keeping him cool on the way to the show. Keep as much of the worry in my pocket and out of his. I didn't say a word, only remembered the ones that Skip had put in my ear. *Keep him cool, Weary. That's as much a part of your job as anything else.*

"Heard a rumor going around that your Dodgers might leave Brooklyn, head out this way. You won't have to watch the Hollywood Stars and pretend like it's real baseball."

"That'll be a sight. Los Angeles Dodgers."

"You can sing the national anthem. Maybe they'll have an organ like your team back in Chicago."

"I'll leave that to a youngster. I'll be on the third-base line somewhere watching."

His hands started to get quiet, and that was a good thing. They'd be on that piano soon enough.

"They keep saying I'm making history, Weary. Strange thing to call it when it's still in front of me."

"The kind you make for yourself, though. The best kind."

People kept telling him he was the first of us, and that he made them proud. I think he'd heard "the Jackie Robinson of television" one time too many. People meant well, but that was a lot of weight to carry, especially for a showman who needed to have some bounce in his step.

"Come a long way from Montgomery, say friend?" he said.

"You and me both."

He did that last bit of humming then, and the sound came through warm vocal cords, neither tight nor nervous. He looked at that clock one last time, aware of how close he was, so that when the knock came he was good and ready to go.

The National Broadcasting Company proudly presents. Then the drumroll took over and the crown began to spin. *The Nat King Cole Show.* And the applause loaded up on the reel-to-reel flowed out of a speaker and into a microphone. We had been told not to clap along, so the applause filled a room of silent gazers. The show started in the shadows, and then the lights came up and caught the edges of Nat's suit first and then his face. Once his new city was alive with lights and stars falling all around his mountain, he started with his questions.

In the evenings may I come and sing to you?
All the songs that I would like to bring to you?

His first show played out like *This Is Your Life* in reverse. He started at the microphone, where he'd gotten famous, with the swell of his orchestra coming from the wings. When his singing was done, he ended where his career started, on the piano. The mirror did exactly what they hoped it would as the camera tightened on that flurry Nat made with his fingers.

The monitors showed us what anyone watching would see, and television could give the viewers what a live show could not. No front-row ticket in any theater could have gotten us that close. His hands filled the frame. Anybody watching saw those notes rising the very second they left his fingertips.

When his hands were finished it was our turn. We held our clapping until he was off the air and the mike was cold. Applause felt too simple an offering after a show like that. Two hands together over and over didn't square with what his fingers had spun for us. Some whistled, and the seated folks rose, as all of us stretched that applause until Nat, with a bow and thank-you, brought it to a close.

With enough applause a show might keep going, but television had no encores. NBC had sales meetings that lasted longer than the show did. They had disappeared into the office suite, the lot of them, Carlos Gastel, Bob Henry, Nat, and all manner of NBC folks.

"I'd like to imagine they loved it." That's what he told me when he got to the car. "They told me to wait for Nielsen."

"Who?"

It never occurred to me how they counted viewers. No ticket stub, no cover charge, or no bar tab, so the old ways to know the tally didn't apply. The ratings company had a list of people who would write down what they watched, and then the people of NBC would know if they had a hit or not. Nat's audience was a mystery until word came down from Nielsen. The pitfall of television was that everyone could see him at once, but he could see no one in return.

While we drove home, through the night-lit neighborhoods between Burbank and Hancock Park, I imagined the Nielsen families hunkered over coffee tables, gathering their thoughts and filling diaries. Whoever they were, they mattered, and they joined the growing ranks of those who could tell Nat King Cole how long this affair might last.

Chapter 14

Montgomery

DAY OF THE SHOW
2:30 P.M.

I had heard Nat sing at Capitol and at NBC, and now I was back in the building where I had heard his first show. The studios' walls were tailor-made for voices, but the Centennial's were not. Some of the sound would make it through the old windows and down the vents. In a place Nat Cole had outgrown, that extra sound would spill down onto the Hill corner. The folks on the street could say they heard it, too.

The Centennial Hotel had thirty-two rooms. Twenty rooms on the second floor and twelve on the third, including the four corner suites. The fourth floor had a rooftop garden on the south end, and the inside area was nothing but the ballroom, with a dance floor and double-sized rafters that held up the roof without pillars that would block the view of the stage. Every seat was a good one.

The New Collegians' bandstand looked like city blocks, with row houses and storefronts stamped into sheets of tin. The roof tiles and windows, and even the wood grain on the front, had been etched onto the metal. The blocks had been quilted together, some looked like New York and others Chicago, a sideways totem to the cities they'd toured.

I walked to the back of the place, where the standing-room folks would hear the show.

"How does it sound from there?"

"Just like you're in the front row," I said.

From the back corner, one could see every bit of the stage, from the piano in the left-hand corner to the row where the percussionists played. I had heard enough shows up there to know how the sound wrapped around the place. Every eye and ear got the same kind of sound.

A few modest steps led from the main floor up the back and the sides, and the elevation gave everyone a good line of sight. No one would crane his neck to get a good look at the stage. If people moved their heads, it would be because the music told them to.

"We hope the stage is big enough," Miss Vee said.

Nat tapped his foot. "Surely. And more solid than most."

"We'll shut down the elevator before the show begins.

People can walk up the stairwell if they want standing room. We run wires down the shaft to the lounge speakers. Everybody in the place will hear you. I know you're used to more with television and all, but we have a good space."

"A studio's nothing but an empty room. They don't have anything on you, Mrs. Varner. How you fill the room is the thing. We have a good stage and a nice place to rest until the show starts. It doesn't take much more than that."

Miss Vee seemed relieved when he said as much, even thankful.

The only sound just then came from the elevator. The two light tolls filled the space followed by the quick steps of the young lady carrying a tray around the corner. When she first saw Nat she changed her step, not quite freezing but taking a pause.

"Thank you, Sonya. You can bring it on down here. Mr. Weary, you come on back, too," Miss Vee said.

Sonya had her eyes on Nat still. Maybe she didn't know about the show yet, or maybe it hadn't been real until she'd seen him. Even with that little bit of shock, she kept the tray steady, and not a drop of liquor wasted. What she carried in those glasses swirled a bit, and as I walked over with her, I got a good whiff of what she'd brought us, three whiskeys from the Majestic, before she set the tray on a table near the stage.

"I asked Mr. Weary what you drink, and I took the liberty and asked Sonya to bring something. I don't partake in the evenings during the show, but I like to raise a glass when I can. Welcome's not official until you toast with your company."

Sonya had not moved. She stood rocking from her toes to her heels and back again, clinching her fingers the whole while. Mrs. Varner gave her a look.

"Well, it'll kill you if you don't ask him, Sonya, so go ahead."

She rested her feet and breathed one good time.

"Mr. Cole, I figured you might want to check the sound in the room and all—"

I was thinking, *Lord, please don't let this girl start singing.*

"—most of the singers do when they come. Well—"

If she does start singing, please let her sound decent or at the very least sing something short.

"Well, my birthday's coming up, and if it doesn't really matter what you sing, you might as well sing 'Happy Birthday' for me when the band comes."

He swirled that little bit of scotch in his glass, and I knew what he was going to say before he said it.

"Why wait for sound check? I can go ahead and sing it right now."

"I was hoping you'd say that."

And Nat Cole did just that and filled the room with that

simple little song. Sonya listened and started rocking so, that I was afraid she might fall backward. She opened her eyes and closed them, almost as if she had taken that first eyeful of Nat Cole singing, stored it away, and come back for the rest of it.

I tried to remember the old birthday parties in Bel-Air, every one exactly the same. No matter the year or the child, we had sheet cake and a spoonful of neapolitan ice cream. Nat had surely been there. He'd sung that song live on television for President Eisenhower's birthday, and he sang that same rendition to the young lady who'd brought our drinks. With no cake and no candles, all Sonya could do was clap.

"What day is your birthday?"

"August tenth," she said. I wouldn't call that look on her face sheepish, but it was honest. "You'll be long gone by then so it was now or never. I thank y'all."

She collected our glasses and picked up her tray with a little bit of flair in her hands and step. "Can I bring you all anything else?"

"No, Sonya. But thank you," Miss Vee said.

I handed Sonya a little of the tip money as she passed me, and she took it in stride and nodded me a thank-you.

"That child had been asking me since I told her you all were coming. I said she could come up and ask you her-self. I guess it never hurts."

"She was right. I needed to see how the room sounds so I might as well sing something useful. The echo is not bad, and once the room fills it'll be perfect."

Miss Vee excused herself and left us with the sound of her shoes as she walked toward the elevator and the ring of those bells as the doors closed behind her.

"Sounds just like it did way back when," he said.

Between the time when the doors opened and he walked onstage, four hundred people would fill those chairs, almost double the size of the colored section at the Empire. The number mattered. Nobody would ration him to his own folks. Nobody would have to wait until he came back across town for a second show. If the room filled up, then he was on the radio. The listeners could drink downstairs or drink at home and make a party of their own. No interruptions this time. I had given up everything for a show that had ended too quickly, so I had built this new life around making it so. If the marquee had room enough for another line beneath his name, I would have had them add one more. NAT KING COLE. GUARANTEED.

Chapter 15

It was too early to see which way the sky would turn. Mornings in Los Angeles were all kinds of dingy until the sunlight and the wind did their cleaning. The quiet made up for it, though. I had the last of my coffee on the porch, where I could read my paper and get a handle on the day that waited for me. The paperboy was on his way down the block. At least I thought as much, until I saw that the rider of the orange bicycle was a woman. She threw papers on the other side of Seventy-Fourth Street before she made a U-turn at the Avalon corner.

I'd seen her a few times before in my weeks driving around Central Avenue. She sometimes rode with two children, a boy and a girl, whom I had seen rolling newspapers in front of that storefront next to the Dunbar. The bicycle the woman rode, orange with whitewall tires, was one of those I saw leaning on a telegraph pole in front of that newspaper office. The baskets had tin placards with

the same lettering as in the storefront window. LOS ANGE-
LES TRIBUNE, DELIVERED EVERY THURSDAY.

Traffic got heavy at that hour of the morning with the
sidewalks full of students and teachers headed to the
grammar school up on Sixty-Sixth. As the woman on
the bicycle slowed, she spoke to the crossing guard and
tossed a paper to her. She rode toward me, throwing the
paper to the neighbors' houses with an overhand that had
enough arc to find the front walk. She wore those pants
that I'd seen the women in. My sister called them pedal
pushers, but how high-water pants came into fashion was
beyond me.

"Good morning, Mr. Weary. When I saw your name on
the subscription card, I decided to stop and say hello if I
saw you. And here you are. I like to welcome newcomers.
Especially somebody coming here from Alabama."

I knew good and well that my subscription card didn't
say a thing about where I'd come from, and her face was
not familiar. Friendly, surely, but not familiar. Questions
came to mind when a stranger knew my business. I said
my good-morning while I walked to the gate.

"Almena Lomax. *Tribune* editor. On Thursday mornings, I'm director of circulation," she told me. "We're the
third Negro paper in this town. Small family operation.
What we don't have in size, we try to make up for with
customer service. Welcome to Los Angeles."

She motioned to the bicycle she'd just rested against the gate.

"My son and daughter work Towne Avenue from here to Florence, and I cover Avalon to Central. My youngest is barely walking, so she's got some years before she'll be riding. She's with my husband. Likes to sleep in the back of the station wagon while he drives his route."

She had the paper in her left hand and offered her right like the chancellors did at graduation, a diploma in one hand and a shake with the other.

"Thank you, but if we met years ago in Alabama and I don't remember, then I apologize, but ma'am, I have to ask—"

"We haven't met. Ten years ago, we got word on the newswire about a riot in Alabama. Can't always trust the wires, I've found. So I called some of my family around Eufaula, over on the Chattahoochee River. You might have heard of it."

"Been in that river a few times."

"Me and you both, Mr. Weary. Well, I called and they told me it wasn't a riot. My people said a soldier got between Nat Cole and a white man with a pipe. Of course, folks love to embellish a bit. No harm in it. One version of it had you jumping down from the third tier. Throwing chairs and music stands. Is that how it happened?"

"I was warned against correcting folks."

"I wish the rest of it were false. The Kilby part and that time they gave you."

"It's behind me now, Mrs. Lomax."

She was a stranger to me, but a sincere one. Still, though, she was a journalist, and the last time I had been in the paper, my name was turned to scandal. So I didn't need to be anywhere close to a front page unless I was reading it at breakfast.

With Mrs. Lomax off that bicycle, she seemed ready to talk for a while. Getting into folks' business was her trade and craft. All the same, it was all kinds of wrong to leave a woman standing and me not offer her a seat, so I did.

"No, thank you. I ride thirty or so blocks on Thursdays, so standing's not a problem. I just want to let you know a few people out here remember your name. Nat Cole included, it seems. He was a smart man to hire you."

She looked me over after saying as much, studying. Maybe she thought my face would answer her question before she asked it. But I had learned to put a little more stone in my face.

"Mr. Weary, you being hired by Nat Cole isn't exactly a secret. Just like Augustine Tate was a prizefighter. Half the drivers and bodyguards were boxers. The rest, the ones like you, have a fighter's sensibility. That look

on your face might make a troublesome man think twice
before he jumps a stage."

All I could say was maybe, because it was no telling
what a man might do.

"In any case, I'm not looking for information on your
employer. I'm more interested in what I've been hearing
about the situation in Montgomery. The busses. Have you
heard anything about the busses?"

She studied my face some more, trying to read what I
hadn't said yet. I was careful about my hands giving me
away. That newspaper was nothing more than something
to twist or hold too tightly. It might as well have been a bell.

"It would be better if I kept my name out of anybody's
paper."

"It's not anybody's paper, Mr. Weary, it's mine. It's just
that I only know a handful of folks in Montgomery. Great-
aunts and distant cousins can only get me so far. I need a
few more folks I can call. Just like I imagine you have to
learn your way around Los Angeles."

I nodded then.

"Claudette Colvin was the young lady arrested back in
March. You know her?"

"Some of her people. Montgomery's only so big."

"I was here trying to write about her from two thousand
miles away. Posed some difficulties."

"More like twenty-two hundred and some change."

"All the more reason to make friends in Montgomery."

She looked back and saw my neighbor on his front porch. He had been fighting a losing battle with the squirrels that emptied his bird feeder, and he'd tied all manner of wire to keep them off. He was trying wind chimes now, and Mrs. Lomax turned around when she heard the racket he was making with his pliers.

"Looks like an *Eagle* under his bushes. Good way to lose readers, putting a newspaper in the dirt. Excuse me for a second."

Mrs. Lomax wiped her fingers on the rawhide flap of the news bag like a pitcher fingering the rosin. She threw the paper sidearm, splitting the telegraph pole and the apricot tree, planting the *Tribune* in the middle of the porch.

"What's his name?"

"Upshaw. Cyrus Upshaw."

She raised her voice just short of yelling and gave him a nice wave while she said her hello. He waved back, but that look on his face had some confusion in it. He had no idea who she was. But he walked over and got his paper, settled onto his porch swing, and put his head in that front page I still held rolled in my hand.

"I'm also in charge of marketing. I have people in Louisiana, too. Down that way they have a word for what I gave Mr. Upshaw—"

"—a lagniappe. Something on the house."

"Exactly. I hear that word more here than I heard it down south. Half the people here come from back home. I wrote a story last year about the black folks in Baton Rouge boycotting their busses. What happens back home happens here, so I need people in both places. Folks who I can trust, and ones who trust me right back."

"Considering where I been, me and trust have been apart for quite a while. I learned to live without it."

"I can't say I blame you. You don't know me after all."

She looked down then, and her eyes and her hand searched through that bag.

"In any case, I wanted to give you something else."

She checked her fingers for ink, and wiped them against the leather again. She pulled out another paper, yellowed, and handed it to me. The headline stretched across the top, as big as the name of the paper. "Soldier Saves Cole from White Mob." The photograph of me beneath the headline was the same size as the one of Nat.

"Where'd you find this picture?"

"I called the yearbook office at Alabama State College. They gave me the number to that little portrait studio on Thurman Street that took the school pictures. I offered to buy a copy, but they gave it to me free. Said it was the least they could do for you."

"The last time most people saw my face was when the white paper ran my mug shot."

The college sophomore version of me in that picture was a long time gone. Driving a cab had put a little money in his pocket, enough to buy a decent tweed jacket and that tie.

"Police send the booking photos for free. I could have gotten that one, but when some people see you holding a number across your chest, they assume you did something wrong."

The picture was only the half. The story ran onto the next page, underneath a cartoon drawing of a man, me, with outsized fists, a starburst where my knuckles had lifted the attacker's chin. Nat had his head back, singing with his eyes closed, and a small constellation of notes floated in the limelight. In that version of things at least, the show never stopped.

The paper wasn't shaking in my hands, so the trembling I felt was still on the inside. To see the truth in my hands, without having to say it, without having to plead my case or look at a judge, was a brand-new feeling. Something warm on my neck where all that weight had been.

"Do you have any more papers?"

"Which ones?"

"The last ten years."

She looked at me, not searching my face anymore though, just watching me while I held the two papers she'd brought.

"I was on a road crew at Kilby. Every once in a while we'd find a piece of newspaper somebody threw out. I went ten years without reading a paper front to back. I got some catching up to do so I can know where I am."

She had her arms folded, and breathed into a nod.

"We get each year's worth hardbound and keep them next door to our office. I call it a library, but it's a storeroom on the second floor of the Dunbar. You're welcome there any time."

I nodded, and I believe I said thank you, but she had caught me off guard. It was hard to hear my own words in the middle of seeing that school picture. That day was too far gone to remember.

"That's why I'm asking, Mr. Weary. I don't want to be in your business, but it feels like the busses are everybody's business."

I don't know why I looked around before I said it, but I'd never been one for loose-mouth talking and putting business in the street.

"I have a sister on the Women's Council. My brother helped to start the Taxi Guild. You give them a holler, and they might tell you something."

Mrs. Lomax reached into that bag again and pulled out a notepad, flipped to the first clean page, and wrote down the names and numbers I gave her.

"Make sure you tell them I gave you their names. They'll trust you then."

"I will indeed."

Her son and daughter rode down Towne Avenue and stopped to talk to a man and woman, schoolteachers it seemed, walking among the children toward the school. They looked down the block to their mother, who pointed to her wrist, though she wore no watch. The first of the school bells, the ten-minute warning, came ringing out. Mrs. Lomax's son gave a boy a ride on his handlebars, and her daughter rode beside a group of girls with saddle oxfords on their feet and gym shoes around their shoulders.

"I hope I didn't hold you too long, Mr. Weary. Wouldn't want to keep you from Mr. Cole. Where are you all off to today?"

"I don't talk about my work."

"Like I said, I'd be the last to dig for dirt on Nat Cole. I admit we've been hard on him, but we've been hard on all of the singers. He shouldn't have been singing in a Jim Crow theater in the first place. Don't sing to a crowd you can't sit in, it's as simple as that."

"I guess television changes all that. Sing to everybody all at once. Jackie Robinson of television is what they're calling him."

"Nothing wrong with Jackie, but a Willie Mays of television is what we need. They say Mays could catch hell in his glove if he got a good jump on it."

With that she was back on her bicycle and riding toward Avalon. I lost her behind the cars and the few scattered trees, but the flight of her papers marked her path along Seventy-Fourth Street, as a week's worth of headlines landed on those doorsteps. It was a mighty good notion, knowing that in the middle of her brand-new news she had brought me a little bit of my old time. And I didn't have to track through my mind to reach Montgomery. I could read about it on my front porch.

Chapter 16

"Got a call from your reporter friend last week. Said her name was Lomax," Marie said.

"I was supposed to call you first. I intended to. You were nice to her I hope."

"When have I not been nice? So I need a stranger to remind my brother he has people back here who want to hear from him every once in a while?"

Marie's voice came from a familiar place. She and Pete had moved in with my father a few years back. Her children made the same noise we had in those rooms. The echoes didn't change.

"As much as I call, I never catch you at home. How are you, dear heart?"

"Fine. It's not hard to keep busy, so I do."

"That's the best thing to be."

Every so often the house on the other end went quiet. Marie must have placed a hand over the receiver while she corrected the children. The room would be quieter when she spoke again. I didn't mind a bit of noise, though. It saved me the trouble of asking if the kids were fine, since I heard for myself.

"Nat Cole from up the street on television. And you out there with him. Folks are talking about it. Next best thing to a real show."

"What you think?"

"You know I could listen to that man forever. I'll have to miss the next one. We have a meeting Monday night about the busses. They arrested another woman on the City Lines. A seamstress at Montgomery Fair. Yesterday. Took her to jail right in front of her job."

"They hurt her?"

"People who saw it said no. Your friend Mrs. Lomax wanted a phone call when something happened. And it just did."

Montgomery Fair was just across from the Court Square Fountain, where the biggest Christmas tree in Alabama was always lit the Friday after Thanksgiving. The bell ringers were out, and Santa Claus had a throne set up in the front lobby, with lines of white children wrapped around the place. Half the downtown busses had stops at Court Square, so there might have been as many people waiting for the bus as riding it. When they arrested Rosa Parks, half of Montgomery was probably downtown.

When I drove in college, I'd circle the fountain looking for fares every Friday, weaving in and out of those busses. They kept up a racket, with every piece of loose metal rattling on the Court Square cobblestones. A cab was more money, but for some folks it was worth it, because the busses never had enough back seats. So a Negro rider might wait an hour just for standing room. The folks waiting downtown tried to look dignified when the drivers treated them any kind of way. Maybe it was worth the extra money of taxi fare. Taking a private ride with us was insurance against insult and embarrassment on the City Lines in the busiest part of town.

"We told everybody to stop riding tomorrow."

I knew plenty of people who had sworn off the City Lines, but it was hard to imagine everybody doing so at once.

"I'm more relieved than anything. Been planning for a while, and now it's here. Maybe it's wrong to say I'm excited, because I didn't have to go down to jail. It's just about time, that's all."

"You all need to be careful."

"Too late for careful," she said. "Me and Pete volunteered to run a carpool out of the lot."

"Like I said, be careful."

"So you told me. Been tiptoeing around this sorry town all these years and got squat to show for it."

That house was half-filled with our old furniture and some good, sturdy pieces she and Pete had built and covered. Two of the old living room chairs sat in front of shelves of books and records. Marie and Pete had me over before I left, and I'd drank plenty of their gin. Those chairs flanked the brass telephone table. Since she knew phone numbers by heart, she didn't need her phone book. Instead, it doubled as a coaster, and the sweat rings from the tumblers had changed the yellow of the cover to some shade of gold.

"What did he sing?"

When I told her the four songs, she hummed the first line or two of each. "I've Grown Accustomed to Her Face" sounded good coming through the phone.

"Can't understand why it's fifteen minutes. Milton Berle's got the whole hour."

"Milton Berle's got a sponsor."

"Well, if I can't hear Nat Cole from up the street on television, then I'll hear him tonight. Hold on."

Her voice changed, moving around when she shifted that phone on her shoulder. The albums were alphabetized, a chore for the children they turned into a game. The "C" section stood upright between a set of cast-iron jacks, and it had every one of Nat's albums along with Ray Charles and Ida Cox.

When I had been there with them, I'd put some hours

into listening on that hi-fi, sitting in that very chair, staring into the speakers, because what came out was clearer than anything I had ever heard. Some were on the charts and some years old, but they were new to me, like the needle had hit the vinyl while it was still warm from the press. I had left a few dimes for the children, pay for rearranging the records, so when my sister reached for an album, she knew exactly where it was.

"No 'Christmas Song'?"

"Two weeks from tomorrow. He's saving it."

And no sooner than I said as much did the swell of those strings come up.

"I can't wait two weeks to hear my song. After the weekend we had down here, two weeks seems like forever. No business waiting for my show and crying about missing it. I can hear it right now."

"Crazy thing is I'll never see it on television."

"You won't miss a thing. You'll be in the room when he's making it. That's a show on top of a show."

Marie swirled that ice in her glass.

"I'm supposed to be at the gas station early. Watch the bus stop across the street to see how many get on. It's Monday, too. So the laundry girls will be waiting for that five o'clock bus. We got rides ready to go. The Lord may find it peculiar, but we'll all be praying for empty busses. Dirty smoke and squeaking doors and all the rest."

Sometimes I was glad to be rid of my hometown, but leaving and forgetting are nowhere close to being the same. I thought about home when Marie covered the phone and said good night to the kids. Her fingers weren't enough to muffle my name, Uncle Nathaniel, as they told her to tell me good night. And even if a part of me hated that place, my people were in the middle of it.

"I told your friend to keep my name out of the paper. I could put her in touch with—with the executive committee."

"You can say her name. I won't fall to pieces hearing you say something about Mattie. She's your friend."

"You know, when that reporter called, knowing your name and everything, I thought she was your friend. Your *friend* friend."

"Mrs. Lomax. That means married. With a bunch of kids."

"She told me that, too. Not her then, but somebody, eventually."

"I'm out here making Los Angeles feel like home. Turning strangers into friends."

"I'm talking about finding one somebody."

Truth was, I found me a few somebodies, just like I had at Mama Nonie's. Los Angeles was a place full of strangers, and I made the most of it. I could be a brand-new man every other night or so. Let a woman call me by a borrowed name. It didn't matter that she forgot it as soon as I was dressed and gone, because I forgot hers as well. The part of my mind where I did my loving and remembering had been cut back to the root. It would come back, eventually, but until then all I could handle was the skin-deep loving that I paid good money for.

"Everything's fine. If not, it will be eventually," I told her.

"That shows what kind of kin we are, dear heart. That's my resolution. Not just New Year's but from here on out. Make everything fine sooner or later."

She was right about us being kindred as much in spirit as in blood. I drank some of the same liquor she and Pete had toasted me with before I left for California. And sitting there by my lonesome, I listened to the same music she had spinning back home.

Chapter 17

Being the driver of a Capitol Records star meant I could take a seat in the Studio A lounge in the back row of seats behind the audio board. At the first of Nat's December sessions, a ten-minute break had stretched to half an hour on account of the squeak an engineer heard coming from one of the orchestra's chairs. A stray noise could kill a song as fast as a scratch ruined vinyl. Nat's engineer wore his headphones, listening as a maintenance man went down the rows and tested chairs with his weight. Each time Manny shook his head, the fellow moved on to the next one.

The folks from duplication made copies of the scores for the band, and they had come down from the fifth floor with a few handfuls of music changes. That was my first time seeing the two Negro transcriptionists, a woman and a man. As a general rule, I nodded to the other black folks in the place, whether I knew them or not. Nothing wrong with having a little company. Johnny Mercer sang about enough of us before he built Capitol, so it stood to reason that he should hire a few.

The two of them passed sheet music along the rows nearest to me. The man nodded my way, and even though he looked familiar, I didn't know for sure. By the time he walked over to me, I remembered him. He had played the trombone with the New Collegians that night back in Montgomery.

"We never met back then, at least not proper like. Willie Walker," he said. "Figured I'd see Nat Weary around here sooner than later. I heard Mr. Cole hired you."

"Got out here a few weeks ago."

"I got out here a week after that show."

Last time I saw him, he was holding a piece of horn in each hand behind the Empire's screen, his trombone slide bent to hell. He shook my hand like we'd been friends for all those years.

"My cousin drove me to Mobile that night. I was on that Sunset that next morning and been here ever since," he said. "Bust a white man across the head with a trombone and it's time to hit the road."

"I should have been right behind you."

"Nat put in a word for me when I got the nerve to ask him. I was working at a record shop around the corner from the old building on Sunset. That's where me and my Evelyn met."

He waved toward her, and once she'd emptied her hands of the sheet music, she joined us. She had a little bit of jewelry on her, a silver bracelet and two rings on her left hand. My Evelyn, he called her, with a little swell in his throat when he said it. His arm brushed her elbow as he introduced me.

"Baby, this is the fellow from that night back home, Nathaniel Weary."

"So you're the one. The fellow from up in the balcony. Figure your ears have been burning all these years as much as you've been talked about."

They both wore glasses like most everyone in the department did. A lifetime of small notes in bad light, and the eyes could take only so much. He had the round sort and hers were pointed. She wrapped both of her hands around mine and squeezed, her shake as warm as the hello was. The charms on her bracelet were typewriter keys, mother-of-pearl with letters, a number or two. Evelyn was the kind of California woman a country boy would fall for. She had as much city in her talk and her smile as she had down-home. Los Angeles with a little East Texas sweet. From Tyler, she told me.

"Sinatra and his people come through tomorrow. Got

a bit of work to finish so we can split at a decent hour. Me and Evelyn work another little job, a midnight show tonight down at John Dolphin's place, the one on Vernon. Come on down if you're off the clock."

"Should be all done," I told him. "I can hear you play that horn again."

That look told me I'd just said something wrong. It was that bit of squinting he did, looking at something that was in his head.

"I moved on from my horn."

He searched for something to say next, but Evelyn rescued him.

"We'll save you a table tonight," she said, and he jumped in and repeated the same.

Manny finally raised a finger, and the man from maintenance ushered out the guilty chair, third from the right in the string section, probably to the cafeteria or the secretarial pool, where noises were too common to cause notice. Manny eased off the earphones. When he opened the mikes, the flood of studio noise came into the booth. Nelson Riddle called the orchestra back, and the musicians on the hallway phones filed back in. Nelson and Nat weren't big on wasting time. Quiet chairs and new music, the duplication folks left, and Willie and Evelyn headed for the door. Then it was just me and Manny.

"I asked Willie about his horn and I must have said something wrong."

Manny swiveled his chair around.

"Way I heard it, Willie got hit in the jaw with something at that Alabama show, and he couldn't get right after. Shame, I heard he was pretty good."

"He was," I said. And I was hearing "Tuxedo Junction" again, a horn player's song if there ever was one, that trombone right next to the trumpet from the start. Everybody in the place swinging like they did.

Back on the other side of the glass, Willie said good-bye to the trombonists, Shorty and Juan. A little word and a laugh with his people. He said he had moved on from his horn, but I knew it didn't work that way. He was comfortable around those horn players, but no seat waited for him. A horn player needed a fighter's jaw, strong as the steel it was working. A little talk with his kindred during a break was as close as Willie could get to his old time.

"When Skip used to sit back here he told me that story. Soldier from Alabama. You hit that man with a chair from the bandstand the way I heard it."

"If I could have dropped that Steinway on his ass, I would have."

"Be better off with a Hammond organ," he said. "B3. It's portable. Easier to handle."

By then the players had taken their seats, and Nat had left the piano bench for his stool and his microphone. Manny picked up the headphones again. I liked to take a look at the reels of fresh tape turning behind me when the band started to play, seeing where that music was headed once it left those sheets.

Willie and Evelyn stood next to the blue Skylark in the east end of the parking lot. I hadn't known who it belonged to, but I'd seen the car every day with the top down, ready to make the best of quitting-time weather. Evelyn had the trunk open and stood there with another handful of papers. Instead of sheet music, this time she carried blue-and-green flyers no bigger than note cards with dolphins and microphones swimming around one another.

"We'll be looking for you tonight, Weary," she said, handing a card to me. "Show one of these at the door, and you get a drink on the house."

Willie was over by the Vine Street sidewalk, next to one of the security guards and a couple of delivery drivers who all held the same little flyer I did.

"If I'd known, I wouldn't have said anything about Willie's horn."

"No need to be sorry. It wasn't your doing. Besides, we

know Skip from when he drove for Nat. He told us where you've been all this time."

She leaned back against the open trunk, looking toward Willie. Some tourists were near them, pointing cameras toward the steeple. One asked the guard a question, directions it seemed like, and he pointed, then cupped his hands westward. Grauman's Chinese maybe, handprints in the concrete.

"Never heard him play his horn, but Willie's the best 'bone player I know. Maybe that's love talking, but there's no harm in that," she said.

"He played 'Tuxedo Junction' better than the boys in Birmingham," I told her. "God's honest."

"I don't doubt it for a minute," she said. "We'll raise us some glasses tonight at Dolphin's, my friend."

Willie came back around. He wore a short-brim Kangol, lifted enough to wipe his forehead. Going from that air conditioning to the street would bring that sweat out in a heartbeat.

"Got to show you something before you go."

He turned one of the cases in the trunk sideways and flipped the lid open. Nestled in a little velvet-covered frame were two microphones, arranged head to tail.

"Philmore," he said. "Lollipop mikes they call 'em. Just like what you whipped that man with."

He gave one to me, and the microphone felt about right

in my hand. I remembered the weight of it but not the look, because I was grabbing halfway blind and keeping my eyes on that pipe. The cloth cord had tangled around my wrist, and I remembered the electric buzz that went dead when the microphone broke to pieces on that man's face. I set the Philmore back in the case, and Willie stacked it in the trunk with the rest.

"I was on the floor, trying to get my feet under me so I wouldn't get my head stomped. Didn't see you hit that man, but I damn sure heard him holler," Willie said.

"Some of these boys singing tonight like to throw microphones on the floor," Evelyn told me. "The way you hold it, you might have some R and B in your veins."

"I can't carry a tune."

"Neither can most."

They got in their car, the seats, the piping, and the dashboard a couple of different blues. With the top down they'd be riding with the sky color underfoot and all around. Evelyn rubbed her hands along the headrest, settling in.

"So long, Weary. Until this evening," Willie said, raising his voice above the turn of the engine.

Chapter 18

I sat at the bar while Evelyn and Willie ran microphone wires around the baseboards of John Dolphin's place, from the stage to the homemade sound booth, a banquette and two tables pulled together off to the side. Dynamite Jackson ran the bar on the second floor of Dolphin's building on Vernon Avenue. The back windows looked out onto his car lot, where every convertible's top was down, every hood up, and every door open. What Dolphin didn't make in car sales he made up for in records and live shows.

The house band had trickled in, crowded around bottles of Pabst Blue Ribbon. The drums were next to the piano, and two Regal cases sat against the speaker. A Fender bass against the wall. The organist screwed the legs on his Hammond. Manny was right. I could drop it on somebody if I had a mind to.

Dynamite Jackson's back was to me when I answered his question, but he turned around and asked me to repeat myself, as though that mirror behind his liquor had twisted my words around. He swallowed hard, too hard for the smooth liquor we both drank.

"Ten years?" Dynamite said. "Good Lord, man. All this time. For beating a man?"

"Didn't even get to finish," I said.

"Sorry to hear it."

He poured another round. When Dynamite said sorry again, the man three stools down, not quite drunk but on his way, asked who died.

"Nobody, Chester, worry 'bout yours," Dynamite said. "Worry about that tab."

"What you sorry for then?" Chester asked me.

"I was in jail back home."

"Parchman?"

Shook my head.

"Angola?"

"Kilby. Alabama."

"For what?"

"Started a riot."

"Good for you. Need to start one in Mississippi. Yazoo City. Tell them Chester McAfee sent you."

"That's where you left from?" I asked him.

"Yep. I carried my ass on out here in a hurry."

"You keep raising that glass, Chester. You want to buy that man a drink?"

"Then I won't have enough for your tip."

Dynamite had turned the wall behind him into a checkerboard of prizefighters and musicians, hanging pictures from his boxing days and headshots of the singers who'd played there. The poster of Dynamite caught him in his leaner years, lifting his title belt over his head. Heavyweight champion of California. In the others he was face-to-face with half of Murderers' Row, either in the ring sparring or raising a glass at that bar.

Dynamite was one of Skip's old drinking partners, and that was how he got a job with Nat, who'd played that stage every Tuesday way back when.

"So old Nat's on television, now. I'm proud an' all, but he's keeping my Monday-nighters home."

"Fifteen minutes though. Show's over in a jiffy, so anybody who stays home didn't mean to come in the first place."

Evelyn stood at the upright piano, tightening the stand she'd set next to it. Once she was done, she brought the black-and-yellow cords back around to the tables.

"Skip tell you we fought back in thirty-eight?" Dynamite asked me. "Tell you I whipped him like his pop used to?"

"He told me you won by split decision."

"Decision? His knees decided to buckle. His ass decided to hit the canvas. That what he meant by decision?"

Skip's picture was among the boxers on the wall.

Dynamite said that for somebody to get in one of the framed pictures they had to earn it in a boxing ring, on a field, or on a stage. Nat was there below the photograph of Melba Liston holding her trombone, and between two Robinsons, Sugar Ray and Ray Charles. Underneath that glass, the pictures looked a little faded, but they stayed free from any dust or splatters.

When she finished with all the wiring, Evelyn sat next to me at the bar. Willie was still talking to the band, showing them something about the microphones.

"These singers like to roll on the floor, knocking the mikes around. We saved up for those, same kind Nat and Sinatra use, so they don't come a dime a dozen. These boys need to get famous first, because if the mike gets busted, nobody can hear them holler."

She said the singer was new in town, a fellow named Dale Cook out of Chicago. All Dynamite and Evelyn knew was that he had a gospel act with his brothers, but he was solo that night. I'd seen the kid, a teenager it seemed, putting flyers on the door and the notice board out on the sidewalk. Once I could see the face above the name, I realized it was him. LIVE TONIGHT, MR. DALE COOK. Those worn posters had no club's name or date on them, so they worked when he did. He came in and nodded to Dynamite, who pointed toward the band, the Mellow Tones they called themselves, who were over there talking to Willie.

"He looks nice enough, but they all do at first. Then they start doing splits and whatnot, and lo and behold that mike hits the floor and I got headphones full of noise."

"Willie's talking to him, so maybe you'll be all right."

"We lie to them. Say we borrowed Nat Cole's mike and have to get it back safe. Then they sing a little better, like he's on the end of it listening."

Willie set up the stand, and Dale Cook held that microphone, a Neumann, Evelyn called it, said it still smelled like the box. He cradled it like it was too precious to touch the ground, but his grip was hard enough to squeeze the song out of it.

"He's got a good touch. Sometimes I have to give a demonstration. Tell them to hold it like they would a lady's hand at the school dance. Firm and gentle at the same time. But singers, you get all kinds. Everybody doesn't have the same kind of couth."

Dynamite agreed, and he set two drinks down, a Jack Rose for Evelyn and a Seagram's for Willie, who'd come over and taken the corner stool.

"If he sings like he talks this one might be all right," Willie said.

The coasters on the bar were the ones the two of them had brought. W&E LIVE RECORDING. Evelyn raised her drink while she looked toward the door, getting the attention of the woman who'd walked in. I didn't stare, but I wanted to.

Had to. A little piece of that smile she gave Evelyn came my way.

"This is a friend of mine," Evelyn said. "Nathaniel Weary, this is Lucinda Abrams. Lucinda, this is Weary."

The diamonds in that argyle stretched from her shoulder down to her waist. One last cluster dotted the hat she wore just so. I left my stool to shake her hand, and there was that bracelet, the same as Evelyn had. Treble clef and a half note, clicking, just beyond my fingertips.

"Happy to meet you, Weary." She hit a sweet note when she said as much, like she was starting off a song.

"And Miss Abrams, it's a pleasure."

She asked Dynamite for a whiskey I'd never heard of with a little lime and a nice bit of ice. Dynamite measured out that drink, and I did the same with my talk, trying to sound like a whole lot of gentleman and a little touch of friend. Not too common and not too stiff, but smooth enough to sit for a while and let that talk go where it needed to.

"Alabama, Evelyn told me. We're not quite neighbors, but a couple states over, I suppose. West Memphis. Arkansas, not Tennessee."

"What's wrong with Tennessee?"

"About as much as is wrong with Arkansas, but I'm gone now. Been gone for twenty years."

She raised her glass and shook it just so, and that bracelet and the ice moved in the same bit of time.

"Here's to being gone from everywhere but right here," she told me, that free hand pointed down, planting her flag in that little space between her stool and mine. I raised my glass, too, and put a little toast next to hers.

"I'll take being here, right now, over anyplace in the world."

She squeezed three limes into the glass, careful not to let the seeds get past her fingers. Pulp settling into the hollow places in her ice cubes.

"That whiskey is confused."

"No, sir. This whiskey has never had it so good. This California lime's the best thing that ever happened to it. All that time in that barrel, that bottle, and now it's home in this nice glass. A little ice, and fresh air, and a little lime."

"That whiskey might forget it's bourbon."

"Well, friend, it's not bourbon. It's rye. I pulled enough corn when I was a girl that I don't care for anything made from it. No qualms with rye."

Evelyn and Willie had slipped away, across the room to the booth by then, a few last things to do before the music started. Lucinda pointed to the glass, and got Evelyn's attention at the booth. They both raised their glasses, a silent toast halfway across the room.

"When I came in, she gave me the high sign that you were good people. Something we used to do when we were out and about, if we met a couple of boys. A Jack Rose on the rocks means for me to come over in a minute or two. A glass of milk punch means retreat. That meant we needed to cut our losses and start fresh without hurting anybody's feelings."

"It's good to know I passed."

"Nothing wrong with good company."

There was the little thing then, a nudge of my arm and a smile along with it. We left it at that for the moment, because the band needed attention.

"Don't like to have my back to them," she said. "I know the feeling of singing in a new place. Good to see a friendly face or two."

Dale introduced himself, and said he was born in Mississippi, and he got a couple of handclaps. He called out Chicago and got a few more. Wendell Phillips High School, he said, Nat's old stomp. He started his set with a tune from New Orleans, but when the organ started in you could tell he had Chicago in him, too. He wasn't fighting that organ or hiding behind it. No, he climbed right on top as steady as could be. And his voice had two edges to it, a little bit of twist and a whole lot of smooth. What Willie and Evelyn heard through the headsets must have sounded like it needed to, because it sounded fine to me.

Dynamite's walls had no redwood and no panels to catch the sound like Capitol's did, but the walls didn't need them because the place was crowded with people by then and the air was full of smoke and talking. The place had none of that tin can sound, just the sweet noise made in a room full of friends and like-minded strangers. The echoes had no place to bounce, because the sound always found a body or a soft place to fall into. Lucinda probably had a little bit of that sound on her shoulders, or some mixed with that cool water running down the side of her glass.

"I think this Mr. Cook might be all right," Lucinda said, swinging around on that stool, tapping my hand as she told me as much.

"Next time I'll come and hear you sing," I told her.

"You probably already have," she said. "You just didn't know it. Choruses. Bunch of records and a handful of movies. Once upon a time I was all over Europe with Clora Bryant's band. The Sweethearts."

"Where about?"

"A little of everywhere. France mostly."

"I was over for a spell. Uncle Sam."

"So you got to see a bit of the world."

"Got to Paris in the end. Half-drunk and on parade. Still, it looked like a place a man would want to see again."

"Didn't it though? I drank a little champagne everywhere I went. And the be-all, end-all, was that we drank champagne in Champagne," she said.

"That's when you got too refined for corn whiskey?"

She gave me a look then, with a nice bit of salt in it.

"We have to start somewhere, don't we? As long as we end somewhere else," she said.

"And look at me now. I ended up right here next to you, listening to that fellow up there singing that song I haven't heard in a while. Never like that. I'll take this over Paris and Champagne and all the rest of it."

The way it came out, she could have thought it was the liquor talking. Maybe I had misfired and come across as foolish. Maybe I was a milk punch away from sitting alone. She had spooned out a sliver of ice then, and she took it like medicine. And that tightness in her lip was on account of the cold, or me talking my little piece of trash. But I was as serious as the state police, and I told her as much. She thought about it long enough for that ice to turn back to water in her cheek.

"It does sound pretty good. Him singing in one ear, and you and your talk right here. That's why I came to California in the first place. See what I could see, and hear what I could hear."

When the band finished, we moved from the bar to the booth behind Willie and Evelyn, and before the band started to play again, Evelyn handed Lucinda two headsets.

"You ever heard a show like this, Weary?"

"Not yet."

She took off her earrings and set them on the table, and

then she slid the headset on. I did the same. In my time at Capitol and NBC, I had been close to engineers and seen the needles jumping on the gauges, but I had never listened to the show like they had. I closed my eyes and my head was all about the listening. Lucinda knew that song, and when the drummer hit that high hat, she did the same with a light tap on my knuckle, so quick that the feeling stayed longer that her finger did. And that music and that touch got into my head like good liquor, mixing and chasing from the first taste to that last corner.

The candle on the table gave that small circle of light that asks you to lean into the glow of it. The little flame, half drowned in the pool of wax, went up and down like tidewater, and every wave gave Lucinda a new portion of light. And while I loved what I heard from that band, I wondered about her voice, trying to hear it in the songs that came through the headset. I lifted every bit of song from her talk, even that good-bye when we stood outside.

"Until next time," she said.

I told her, respectfully, that I wanted to put next time on my calendar as sure as there was a Friday. I just needed to know where to call. She wrote her phone number on one of Evelyn and Willie's coasters. She waved it between her fingertips, and let that indigo ink from her fountain pen dry in the cool breeze coming down Vernon.

"We can talk about next time," she said.

"I'd love nothing better," I told her. "Good night, Miss Abrams."

"Good night, Weary."

She gave me her hand once again, and it was still warm from the clapping and finger snapping that the music had called for. And I would have walked her home, even if home had been across the water, but she was fine with that cab that stopped as soon as she whistled. And with that she was on her way, and so was I. If I could have, I would have given back the meantime hours between right then and next time, just so we could start it all over.

Chapter 19

Christmas had moved into NBC Studios. Fresh-cut trees and garland had been gathered from some California woods and lay stacked on pushcarts along the backstage corridors. All the sets, whether they were city sidewalks, living rooms, or kitchen tables, had been draped in holiday colors.

The story lines were no different, every romance and comedy skit had had some yuletide sprinkled on it. The rundown for *The Nat King Cole Show* was likewise arranged. Nat had turned a carol into a platinum standard years before. Since millions of folks owned that record, maybe the Nielsen families among them would watch. What the home audience would look like, no one could truly say, but the studio audience would sure enough grow.

Nat would no longer sing to a half-empty studio. Instead of a skeleton crew and a handful of salesmen, he would have a full-fledged audience sitting in the risers the apprentices had set up, ten rows' worth of seats in a horseshoe around the stage. Each chair had a number, and each number was on a list at will call. Nat had set aside two of them for me, the left side of a middle row. A little perk he called it when he asked who I'd give them to.

"Met a girl down at John Dolphin's show, a friend of Evelyn and Willie in transcription. Thing is, I'm supposed to see her Thursday evening, and I don't want to look like I'm trying too hard."

"Don't mess around and look like you're not trying enough, friend."

The parking space we sat in was not our usual on account of the manufactured snow. A truckload of it covered the corner of the lot, tall enough to block our view of the NBC Color City marquee across the street. I had the windows down, and the snow pile smelled like soap and cake batter. I heard it was what they dumped on the fires when the water was low. The wind blew the fumes our way, so I rolled up the windows.

"Figured the women out here are a little different. They like a little more room."

"All that talk saying fools rush in. It's wrong. The fact of the matter is the foolishness comes when you wait too long. I'm not calling you a foolish man, Weary, because I know better. She's seeing you with fresh eyes, so give her a good look."

"A couple of good seats and some good advice on top. I couldn't beat that if I tried."

"Why would you want to?"

I called Lucinda from one of the phone booths near the secretarial pool. The one I called from had been a prop once upon a time, one of the red British numbers that had been fitted with a Bell telephone. In the shows I liked, a phone booth was always something else, a dressing room for superheroes or a trap door for a spy. Always a little adventure. But I was calling a woman I'd just met and barely knew, and asking her to make a little time for me, and that carried a fair bit of intrigue I felt, rehearsing what I might say and those questions getting louder the closer I got to asking them. I shook loose of that feeling and dialed Lucinda's number, and before too long her voice carried me through that hello with that sweet rise and that bit of welcome in her tone.

"I know it's short notice, but I was wondering if you had plans Monday evening."

"There's a little television show that I like on Mondays. One you've heard of."

"I figured I could get you a bit closer. Nat left a couple of tickets, and, well, I thought you might want to watch it here at the studio."

"If I say no, you might have to go to the next girl on your list."

"It's not a list if your name's the only one."

"That's sweet of you, Weary."

"More like selfish. Giving myself an extra chance to see you again before I see you again."

Outside that phone booth window, I caught a short Christmas parade. A cart full of snow and a twined-up tree on a dolly. The other window in that phone booth faced a dark cinder wall. Maybe it was a shop boy who left the white grease pencil, but it had been used to turn those windowpanes into a blackboard lattice inside the red frame. The top note had an arrow to the unlocked coin box, and a courtesy line: Use the nickel. Leave the nickel. How many calls had ridden on the head of that same piece of change? The numbers on the board were leftovers—a seven, a four, and the last little turn of a half-wiped three. I had set Lucinda's number to memory that night she gave it to me. Ever since then I had been itching to dial it, ready to hear her voice, her answer to my invitation.

"Your first Christmas out here away from your people. My people warned me about meeting a man around the holidays. It's winter and folks go out with their pores open, liable to catch something. Like a feeling."

"What's wrong with that?"

"Sometimes nothing. Good to know whether the holiday spirit is coming over you, or you're feeling something that'll stay awhile."

I was out of practice in telling a woman how I felt. I had never lost my sincerity, but I struggled to make it plain and to say it just so. Lucinda was still a lovely stranger. I remembered what Nat told me about fools and their waiting. And I ended that searching for the right and perfect words, because maybe I needed to talk my way toward them.

All manner of lines had been penciled on the phone booth wall. Some looked like scripts and some were little mottos folks like to remember and leave for strangers. If I had to write one, it would be a simple note I tried to remember. *Go ahead and tell her before your nickel runs out.*

"It's not just on account of Christmas. If I didn't have an occasion to call, I'd find one. Start one from scratch. Besides, I know if you're sitting at home Monday night watching television, you'll be thinking about that empty seat that I was trying to save for nobody but you."

"It sounds lonesome when you say it like that."

She was right, and maybe we both thought it over during that little bit of quiet before she gave me an answer.

"Me and you and two good seats. That's an evening," she said.

"That sounds like a yes."

"And a thank-you to boot. I was going to tell you yes from the get-go, but I just wanted to keep you on the phone for a bit. Good to hear your voice. Take it easy, Weary."

That row of phone booths faced the doors where the audience members would enter. On that Monday, I caught sight of Lucinda, a sweater over one arm and waving the other. She walked along the red and green velvet ropes and stood like she was ready in case that camera swung and put her on television. That kiss on my cheek and that "hello, friend" lingered for as long as that perfume did.

Bob Henry greeted the audience and delivered the news, odd to newcomers, that laughter and applause were prohibited during the show. The applause needed to be a particular sort that could be mixed and faded, so they would have to enjoy the show in silence. The moment Nat took the stage was their one and only time for applause, so they should take advantage of it.

Mrs. Cole and the girls stood in the wings, ready for the cue to join Nat at the end of the show. The living room on set was not as fine as theirs, but it looked the part. The mantel was nothing but rectangles of plywood, brick-sized pieces with a little more black paint in the shadow of the grout lines and a touch of silver on the edges, shadow and reflection making it all work. The spotlight would sell it just like the music would, because once Nat sang about an open fire it was easy to see it whether it burned or not.

Roasted chestnuts and Jack Frost and Eskimos were the farthest kind of cry from that California weather, but the song filled the room just the same. That song had come out while I was gone for the world, and it was new to nobody but me. I had worked to turn it into something classic, playing it over and over again on my hi-fi, as I had done with so many tunes that I had missed.

Lucinda swayed a bit, but she watched the sound man and the boom he rolled, lowering the microphone above Nat's head, just out of the frame. With his voice collected by an unseen mike, Nat made freehanded gestures that welcomed, and then he reversed course and crossed his arms, cocked his head as if listening and thinking, as if the lyrics were simply a holiday brainstorm that had just come to mind.

Lucinda sang silently right along with that quiet chorus of folks in the risers, and we watched that glimmer that came from the silver bricks. The light created the make-believe sparks, but the ones beneath her touch were the same kind of electric, the first few crackles of the home fire.

Chapter 20

Montgomery

DAY OF THE SHOW
3:00 P.M.

M iss Vee said two more guests had arrived, and I found them in the ballroom. Before I saw Evelyn and Willie, though, I saw their cases stacked beneath the coat check counter. They'd flown into Mobile to see his people for a few days, and their bags still had the sunburst stickers from Eastern Airlines and tags for Bates Field.

Willie was across the room on a ladder, wrapping his wires around the rafters. The microphone stands lined the far end of the stage. Evelyn sat at the long table next to the coat check where they sold cigarettes and candy bars on show nights. She had arranged the spools of wire, and they spun a little as Willie pulled more slack. While he ran cable, Evelyn wiped down the microphones with a lamb's wool cloth turned dark from her bottle of wintergreen alcohol.

"I almost called you from down in Mobile. I love his people, but there ought to be a rule on how many hours they have to wait before they can hand me another plate."

She told me as much when she came around the table and hugged my neck.

"I bet it was good though," I said.

"You know it was. But still. We'll be down there through the holidays, and I might not make it."

Willie called over from his ladder, said he'd come and speak when he got done. A couple of kids were there with him, setting up stands. They had PROCTOR written on their band jackets, and I remembered the ones who traveled with the New Collegians, underclassmen putting in a year or two of work waiting for a seat to open up in the band.

"You did all right, Weary. Nice room y'all got for us tonight."

"It's not Capitol, but it'll do."

"It's more fun this way, for me at least. I'll go out and buy live records of songs I already have. I like the applause. Good to hear people while they hear it."

"They'll clap for him tonight. Might holler some before it's all over."

Evelyn pointed behind her to the coat check room, twin rows of empty hangers that would be full come evening.

"My first job in show business. Taking hats and over-coats when I was up in Oakland at Slim Jenkins's place. The house band used to make bootleg records after hours. Used the coat room for a booth. It's always been a good side hustle."

Willie set his microphone stands among the rows the proctors had set up, some for the music and others for the mutes. The cables next to Evelyn spun off the spools as Willie pulled a little more slack to get the wires around the rafters alongside the stage.

"People been talking around Capitol. Word is the television show's gone for good. Is it true?"

"I wish it was a lie. A lot of people know?"

"People say it's a hiatus, but that's because they can't call it what it is. Where I come from, when a dog got old somebody would say, 'We drove him out to the country and turned him loose.' I knew good and well they took that dog somewhere and shot it. That's how they do you in show business. They can't call it what it is, but they still do it."

Her hands got quicker as her words did. She took it out on the fingerprints the last singer had left on the chrome. The microphones gleamed then and looked as clean as the wintergreen had them smelling.

"I can't stand television anyway. You see children with the tin cans and the string? That's how the music sounds. Then they make you jump through hoops to get a show."

"After tonight, he'll go to Europe. A good way to start over and come back right."

"What about you, friend? When Nat and Skip hit the road, where does that leave you?"

"I'm leaving for L.A. in the morning. Not sure about things when I get there, but I'll be leaving anyway."

"What's between you and my friend's not my business, but she is my friend."

Evelyn straightened the stacks of coat check cards, quick fingers, like she did when we played spades, the four of us.

"We talked before I left. She asked how I felt about coming back here. I can't say for sure yet."

"All I knew about Montgomery was that Willie left in a hurry. And you. I heard that story for years before we even knew your name."

The proctors had finished their working and held the two microphones Willie had handed them. He looked over to Evelyn, and she held the headphones to her ear and waited for the needle to jump when Willie started testing. Once she nodded to them, she put the set back on the table, but the proctors held the microphones a little longer. I couldn't hear what Willie was saying. Maybe he told some story about the old days. The speakers were off, but the sound board and microphones were on, and that far-off story registered enough to make the needle jump along with the talk and the laughter.

As cool and drafty as it was, Willie had a little sweat on his temples when he came over to us.

"They don't teach them how to hold a mike in music classes. After all that practicing kids do, the singing needs to sound right. Got to."

"Hear that, Weary, it's got to sound right."

"That's why I brought y'all two down here."

"See baby, old Weary's coming up in the world," she told him. "Promoter and whatnot. Told Weary, it took him to get you back to Montgomery."

"I needed to see it again eventually. I guess it might as well be for a show."

Willie looked around the place and then he looked once more. The proctors had by then set out the mutes meant for each trumpet and trombone bell, each one a little dented. The way the New Collegians used them, quieting the music when they needed to, fluttering the notes with those handfuls of metal, was something I'd never seen until I heard them growing up. It had been their custom to pass down the mutes when they graduated. Before he walked over, Willie had flipped a few, checking which one was his back when. He didn't say anything about finding it, so maybe his was long gone.

His might not have made it back from the Empire. The derby mutes looked like helmets for soldiers, and some of them had been. Scrap metal from the First World War that had been reused, getting a new peacetime life letting notes roll around the bowl and then over the brim. Willie made his living listening, and I'm sure he had heard what I had when the fighting started, that clatter behind the backdrop of their music and things hitting the floor.

How could we not hear it still? I hoped for him the same thing I hoped for myself. We would hear the old sound for only a few hours more, until the show gave us a brand-new memory, loud enough to make that long-ago noise nothing more than a whisper.

Chapter 21

The beat of a typewriter came through the telephone line when I answered, and I figured it was Mrs. Lomax before she said hello.

"Good afternoon, Mr. Weary. Just calling to check up on you. Like to keep up with our readers when I can. I'm not big on surveys but a chat is just fine."

"I'm all right, but I wonder if you call everybody who takes that paper?"

"I believe I told you, we're a small press, so what we don't have in circulation we make up for by being hospitable. Plus I wanted to see if you knew what today is."

"Besides the one on the calendar? No ma'am."

"A solid month off the busses. It galls me to hear people call a month an anniversary, so I won't. But Montgomery holds the record now. Baton Rouge stayed off the bus for two weeks when they tried. A month. You're proud of the folks back home I hope."

"I try to keep my hope manageable. I'm game for good news, but if it's bad I'm not surprised."

Her voice was gone again, turned to whoever was beside her. An older child asked a question about a word. Mrs. Lomax said something about a dictionary, then thesaurus, before she spoke into the receiver again.

"Excuse me," she said. "My oldest has a book report. Deadlines all around this evening. I'm filling two holes in my front page. A famous Negro on television and a city full of black folks making waves in your hometown. Fifty-thousand black folks and not a one on the bus. They could fill the Hollywood Bowl a couple of times over."

The numbers mattered to me. Somebody was always counting, keeping track, even when the numbers worked against us. It was good to hear a number that sounded like winning. But it had been one month. Thirty days felt like a triumph until I considered how long things had been the same or getting worse.

"I hope they're ready for what's coming," I told her. "The law back home, they like to make examples of us. I know that for a fact."

"They seem ready. It'll be a long winter for your folks, but I suppose it takes that sometimes."

Montgomery's January was milder than most, but it was winter enough, with plenty of rain to make up for what we didn't have in snow. Going most places was a long-enough walk, made longer by roads with no sidewalks. If the walkers didn't break in the first month, maybe the boycott would stay together. Imagining the empty busses rumbling through Centennial Hill was a good notion, enough to make that cold-weather walking worth the toil.

"Mr. Weary, I'm afraid the newspaper will spend more on long-distance calls than we will for electricity," Mrs. Lomax told me. "I want to thank you for putting me in touch with your people. Problem is the more questions I ask the more I have. So I think it's better for me to ask in person. I'm finishing the paper tonight before I head to the airport in the morning. Montgomery might be home for a while."

"I don't see myself ever going back, and I don't know why you want to, either."

"My work takes me places, Mr. Weary, so it's not always about me wanting to go. Of course, how could I not be a bit curious? If it's over this time next week, I can say I got there in time to see it."

"Those drivers wear uniforms like the screws wore at Kilby. Hats, ties, everything. They even carry the same pistols, right where the whole world can see them when that door opens."

She was quiet for a minute. It took me years to realize that it wasn't normal for bus drivers to carry guns, to pull them when they pleased.

"Be careful. It's a different kind of trouble down there," I said.

"Not exactly different. We had riots here a few years back. During your war. A couple hundred enlisted men, white boys beating and killing people. I reported from my window before they shot it out, then I went on the roof and saw everything. I don't avoid the trouble, but I find a smart place to watch."

She had stopped typing by then, but a faraway typing continued, her child with slower strokes, searching out letters before putting fingers on the keys.

"You know who my father-in-law is, Mr. Weary?"

"I heard his name. Lucius Lomax."

"People like to call him a gangster, but I think that's vulgar. He was a racketeer for a time, no secret to anybody. He said it didn't make much sense for folks to run and buy the *LA Times* to check the numbers when he could sell them his own paper for less. Even if they didn't win, they'd know what's what, maybe read a poem or two after they checked the wire. Mr. Lomax hired me to turn his newsletter into a paper, and I bought this typewriter and all the ones I wore out before this one. Lucius told me fighting back was a repertoire, Mr. Weary. All kinds of ways to do it, your kind and mine being two of his favorite. You don't regret it do you?"

"I miss my years, but it had to be done."

"Those riots weren't stopped by the LAPD. It took so-called gangsters on rooftops shooting into mobs. Good way to see if men are serious about lynching folks is to aim something and fire. Lucius told me a typewriter is a piece of steel that tells people how you feel, but it's not the only tool for such things."

The second typewriter had gone quiet then. Maybe her child was either finished or listening. Both possibly. Maybe one of those typewriters was lightweight and made for traveling. Alabama bound.

She hung up, and it was just me on that kitchen phone. The click of the typewriter was gone, but it stayed in my head, another sound to go with the ringing that had started again. There on my feet I had felt all right, but when I took a seat, the tiredness came over me. It was not from my work. It was just tiresome thinking about folks having to fight for the least little thing. I loved my people for fight-ing, but hated the reason why, and that left me with that crosscut notion of pride and anger pulling in different di-rections, two kinds of muscle fighting for the same piece of bone.

I'm an ex-Southerner who has returned, though this city is not home. My family hails from Galveston and New Orleans on one side, Mobile and Eufaula on the

other. I have seen the good-hearted ways of Montgome-
rians, and I have witnessed the low-down acts they
have endured as they protest the Jim Crow seating on
the City Lines busses. I arrived six weeks after this boy-
cott began, and I intend to print dispatches from Mont-
gomery until this action is over.

Mrs. Lomax didn't waste any time. Her first article from Montgomery, "Dispatches from the Southland," ran in February. She had turned my birthplace and Los Angeles into twin cities. When her readers unfolded their papers, they would see that LA had been ordered to integrate the firehouses, and the people of Montgomery were walking until their city did the same with its busses. The other Negro papers reported, too, but they hadn't sent any journalists, so Mrs. Lomax showed Los Angeles how it felt to live in the middle of that story.

Her photographs gave top billing to an empty City Lines bus, broken-in walking shoes on the tabby sidewalk, and an anonymous car pool. She showed no license plates, and the faces remained in the shadows of the cars, but the rides were full and traveling. She caught a white bus driver staring out that opened door, with his sidearm showing and nobody there to flinch. Any Angeleno reading the *Tribune* knew what the world looked like from a Montgomery sidewalk.

Mrs. Lomax started her days walking with the morning commuters, and she ended them at the mass meetings.

I heard my share of shouting in many a Galveston church on steaming hot Sundays. I quickly forgot those lessons. But the people of Montgomery, for all of their joyful noise, discovered the spiritual value of silence and the grand power of quietude. The Baptists and Methodists of Black Montgomery, exuberant in their evening meetings, seemed to take vows of silence when they walked to work and school. These walkers greeted one another, friends and strangers alike, but when they crossed into Cloverdale, the Garden District, and downtown, they became as quiet as Quakers. The lesson was this: One can shout and sing for only so long, but the quiet sustains. Enemies can only wonder what the silent foe is thinking.

The *Tribune*'s front page wasn't big enough for me. It could have run on past the kitchen table and stretched from wall to wall, and still I would have needed that much more. Even with everything happening in Los Angeles, it was my hometown all over the front page. I had hoped for some time that Los Angeles might cure me of home, but with Alabama all over my table, that long-ago heartache came right on back.

Chapter 22

Montgomery

DAY OF THE SHOW
3:25 P.M.

The boxes behind the front desk held the Centennial's room keys. Box 312 was empty. I had reserved the room for a friend and his wife, so I knew then that they had arrived. I hadn't seen Charles Pettibone since the army, and his invitation was a wartime promise to some of the Alabama soldiers that had taken me eleven years to keep. I'd told them that when it was over and done with, I'd show them a time in Montgomery. Bone remembered that when I called him, laughing all the while he said yes. *Yes, indeed.*

Miss Vee told me the lady was upstairs but the gentleman had gone across the lobby to the Majestic. I wondered if I'd know him by sight. Eleven years was plenty of time to give an old friend a stranger's face, but that voice I couldn't miss.

He talked to Sonya while she tended bar, and she told him she had people down in Marengo. She and Bone called names, saying who had come up from the country and who was still there. I couldn't hear that voice without remembering his yell. Charles Pettibone called the cadence when it was his time to fire, a prelude then a blast, over and over, until that day they were overrun.

Bone had fought with Battery C when he was captured. The forest he used for cover also did him harm. The German shells that hit the Ardennes trees turned the wood to shrapnel. The bits that got into Bone's leg could have killed him, but they left him hobbled instead. The way his foot hung off the bar stool, I could tell it never got all the way right. That leg was good enough to walk on but that twist had healed into the bone. He kept touching that knee, an old habit maybe, or just a case of bone chill brought on by the weather.

The first thing out of his mouth was my name, with that laugh right behind it. I told him to keep his seat, but he paid me no mind. He needed his arms to stand as much as he needed his legs. Eyes, too, it seemed, because he stared at a spot on the floor as he steadied himself on that brass rail. Then he let go of his grip to shake my hand and grab my other arm, kneading it until my shoulder rocked in the joint.

"Look here, Miss Sonya. You see who walked in? Ol' Weary in his good clothes. See? This is citified thread in this Los Angeles suit. Last time I saw you—man—last time was a time."

"Last time's got nothing on this. I'm ready to drink one with Charles Pettibone."

"Like you used to tell it, you drink that good whiskey you can't pronounce. That's saying something 'cause you a college man."

That laugh at the end woke up the place. People looked over, smiling, even though they didn't hear what he said.

"Before we came up, I told Trudy we'd have a nice supper in Montgomery. Kept your secret. Didn't speak his name to a soul," Bone said, his voice low and rumbling. "Trudy likes surprises. I don't on account of my blood pressure. I like to know right off, or at least see it coming. Nice though, ain't it? Knowing something first."

"It is. I'm like you, though. Surprises can go good or bad.

"All Trudy knows is we might hear somebody on the piano."

He said "piano" with that drawl that could squeeze a word, wring out every bit of sound.

"Trudy went to get her coat. We're having lunch with her niece over at the college. She got herself a boyfriend she wants us to meet. He's studying chemistry. A senior.

She said that three or four times on the phone. Senior. Like it's supposed to mean something to me, as long as I been grown. Senior ain't nothing but a year. Young man's distinction."

Bone had on his going-somewhere suit, and his shoes had as much polish as the bar top's stone. His cane was just as clean, carved from the same grade of wood as the wainscot it rested on. Whoever made it had carved leaves and branches, like that cane needed to favor the woods it was cut from. If a man knew he'd need one for the rest of his life, he might as well have one like that.

"Good to get out for a night. Our son and baby girl staying at Trudy's mama's house. She said she could handle two, but not another one. Told me don't bring her daughter home with a souvenir. Said the same thing when we dated. Sweet woman but she can be vulgar. I love her like I love mine, though."

He settled back on that stool then, pointing up to the ceiling.

"He's up there?" He mouthed, "Nat Cole."

I nodded.

"You said you knew him back when, but there's knowing folk and knowing folk."

"I figured it was time for him to come back one last time. Me, too."

"Gone for good. Can't say I blame you."

"I left in a hurry after I got out, but this time I want to leave right. Want it to look like something."

"You always had some style about you. The world is a raggedy-ass place, so any little bit helps."

Bone's hair had turned the same color mine had, gray twisted with black like the herringbone in his blazer. We were equal parts young and old, with our heads keeping tally of the days, the ones gone and the ones we had left.

"Los Angeles," he said, like the name alone was a question. "What you drive him in?"

"Cadillac most days. Imperial from time to time."

"Lord, the choices of a rich man. I'd tell you to drop me off in one and pick me up in the other."

"Might as well."

The sun had tipped a little deeper into afternoon, but the window glaze made the hour feel later. The walking traffic had grown heavier. Children and the schoolteachers had finished their days. Parker's Pharmacy had a line near the ice cream counter. If the boycott had given Montgomery anything, it was a full sidewalk in the afternoons. People had gotten used to taking their time getting to a place, stopping at the High Street windows, doing a little shopping or looking at least.

I had seen enough busses pass to know the schedule. They were few and they were empty, and in that rattle I heard worn metal and broke-down oil. Me and Bone were not Montgomery regulars, so we stared. The people on the street, some with their backs to the busses and some facing them, didn't pay the City Lines any mind.

"Say it might be over soon, but I hope they never go back," I said.

"Don't make any sense though. Customer gives you a dime and you say go to hell."

"What customers?"

"Yes, indeed. Nary a one. 'Cause the customers are gone. In the wind."

He moved his fingers then, like the wind he spoke of needed a little help to blow. He raised his voice when he said it, too. The crowd of folks in there gave us a look then, a longer measure. I didn't mind if Bone got a bit loud, because the last time I heard his voice was in a field hospital. His bed was a few feet away but his voice sounded so much farther, coming at me from the bottom of a well. His eyes were the same way, sunk down low in his skin.

It was good to see him all the way back, with a little muscle in his voice and more weight in his gut. Getting everything back took time if it happened at all.

"Your ears. How they feel?" I said.

"I thought the ringing got better, but a doctor told me I was wrong. Said we just stop remembering how much better things used to sound. Can't worry though. Because when it gets quiet once and for all, that's it. At least for this world."

When Bone raised his glass, I did the same.

I knew the names would come up eventually. It was a gathering meant for more than just us. The boys from Alabama used to drink together. William Pritchett, George Davis, Bone, and me. I made the same promise to them all. *Come to Montgomery, give me a holler, and we'll have a time.*

A farmer near our camp in Tattenhall had given me a bottle, brown liquor without a label. Growing up I'd drunk as much homemade brew as store-bought, but that gift whiskey was different, better than anything I'd had. That man didn't know us, and he was too nice to bring up dying and killing, but I guess he'd watched plenty boys from Tattenhall go off to war. He knew we'd cross that Channel soon and face the same killers his countrymen had.

Bone had had a taste of that whiskey. So had George and Pritchett. We said we'd do it again when the war was over. Some whiskey and a notion. The last I saw of them was when we pulled back and Battery C stayed to cover us. The last Bone saw of them was the day they ran from the prison march.

A driver in an ambulance company told us some of the prisoners from the 333rd were at a field hospital in Liège. We found Bone there. He had spent his winter at the prison on the Nuremberg parade grounds with a broken leg. I was happy to see him alive, because when I had looked at the faces of the boys in Wereth, I thought he was in that pile, too.

"Who made it?" That was the first thing he asked. Half-starved and crippled, he still had his mind on running and the ones who did.

"We found them. They didn't make it."

I couldn't say much else to him. He'd kept them alive all winter in his imagining. His mind was better to them in dreaming than the Germans had been in life. All he needed to know was that they didn't make it. The particulars served nobody but the ones who delighted in our blood. As far as Bone knew, they were shot clean.

"George and Pritchett, and the rest."

We drank our tribute, and gave them their portion when we called the names.

"To the last, Weary."

"The very last."

My mind called the roll, names I hadn't said out loud in years. The problem with quiet was that it opened the wrong door. The one where I'd stacked all that was troublesome.

"If there was something I could have done for you I would have. You know."

Bone knew about Kilby, but I hadn't told him. He had looked me up years before and called the cabstand. When he told my people he was coming to Montgomery, they told him where I was and why. If I had thought he'd call looking for me, I would have told my family to lie to him. He'd lived inside somebody's prison, too, and I didn't want him to feel more weight than he already carried.

"Nothing to do but worry. I had enough folks for that."

"Still. Could have seen you."

"Only thing you could do is this right here. Doing like we said."

Bone had his hand on the bar rail, and his fingers tight on that brass.

"You know I would have busted you out. Hell yes I would."

"Had it all planned out, I bet."

"Yes, indeed. Drive through the gate, that's how they do it in the movies. Saw one the other week at the picture show. They'll have you thinking it's real."

He rolled through the list of names then, like he had a pocketful of Hollywood folks ready to free me. Half were singers, so we'd have a good bit of music to pass our time on the run. We stayed in that story for a minute, and it did us some good, a little salt in that boil to slow down all that bubbling my mind did.

Trudy stood at the top of the Majestic's steps, the front desk traffic passing behind her. I heard Bone easing off that stool, and I stood right along with him. Trudy was as tall as he was, stately, standing there with her jacket on her wrist. They were married before the war, so I had heard her name quite a bit. When we said our hellos, I found out what Bone had told her about me.

"Charles told me you've been in Los Angeles since you came home from Europe. Good to know you like it enough to make it home."

I didn't look at Bone straight-on, but from the corner of my eye I saw he had his head down. Fidgeting with the hat he'd picked up then. Ten years in Los Angeles and no mention of Kilby. He had told his wife a bald-faced lie. I did the same.

"The years have been good. I suppose I have been there long enough to say it's home."

"Good to have you back all the same."

My mother and father told me that a certain kind of friend could get you caught up in a lie, and that lie would tell you all you needed to know about that friend. Charles Pettibone had lied me out of Kilby. Ten years in Los Angeles didn't have to be a lie necessarily. It was just trying the future on to see how it fit. That wasn't a lie any more than trying on a new pair of shoes was lying to your feet. It made sense to see how it felt before claiming it.

"Looking forward to this evening. Said there's a piano player here that's pretty good."

"I believe he'll make a name for himself soon enough."

"Nothing like a night in the city, Nathaniel. Charles and

I thank you for the invitation." That way she said "Charles" made me ashamed to call him by that nickname.

She held his cane and he took her coat, draping it around her shoulders as she put her arms through the sleeves. Then she put an arm under his, helping him stand without too much lifting. The touch did all the work, giving him a bit more balance. We said so long until evening, and they made their way across the lobby and out into the afternoon traffic. I watched them through the Jackson Street windows, heading toward the college, where a niece waited with her boyfriend, anxious and eager to impress.

I had filled two front-row seats with a promise. I needed to set eyes on them, loving folks in plain view. I would listen to Nat's music as I sat near the side of the stage, with my eyes on the shadowy places, but I always got a good look at the front rows. I would listen to Nat and his love songs coming at me sideways in my corner. From there I couldn't help but see the row where I would have been if things had been different.

Chapter 23

We opened Nat's mailbags every Tuesday evening. All of the house staff, "the cohort," as the Coles called us, gathered on the second floor of the carriage house and waited for what I had brought over from the NBC mailroom on Monday after the show. Lottie would leave the kitchen to help us. Elizabeth steamed the rugs on Tuesdays, so while the floors dried she would come over, too. Her husband, Walter, would have finished mowing and edging the front yard by then, and would have set the sprinklers. After a night of watching and walking the grounds, Skip would have had slept for a few hours and have returned to the sorting table as well.

The Coles received more letter openers than one family could use in a lifetime, so we put the surplus to good use. Some were sterling and a few were gold, the same as the records on the wall. Some plain and some initialed. We kept the letter openers in a piece of butcher block that ran the length of the tabletop. Skip stood next to Lottie, rubbing together two of the openers, a matching sterling set with wood on the handles.

"I bet this is how Saint Peter does it. Standing at the pearly gates separating the wheat from the chaff."

"Your priest must get tired of you confessing the same blasphemy week after week," Lottie said.

"It's only blasphemy if it's insincere," he told her. "Wheat from chaff. Sheep from goats."

"Why don't you stop all that talking and give Mr. Weary a hand."

Skip put the letter openers down and took hold of the chain connected to the middle rafter and looped it through the bottom handles of the mailbag. With it hanging upside down over the table, Skip loosened the ties and a foothill of mail rose in front of us.

Nat would answer them when he could, and sometimes we simply pulled an autographed picture from the stacks that never ran out. We kept boxes of 45s to send along as well. If somebody took the time to write a letter, then he might get to listen to a brand-new song before it hit the radio, a little music to go along with a kind word from the man. Congratulations, from Nat King Cole. With thanks, from Nat King Cole. All the best and more, Nat King Cole. The greetings were short but complete. A smile and a thank-you, and that's all most people wanted really. Plus, anyone who would take the time to write a letter would tune in to see the show each week.

Skip and Lottie took the first handfuls, grabbing from the top of the pile only. Letters, I had learned, were just like green groceries, liable to tumble if you disturbed the bottom of the stack. I was five months into it by then, and I had gotten the feel. The rest of them had enough practice behind them to make quick work of it all.

I learned the rules. Never stick your hands into an envelope, they told me. Shake the letters and pictures free. We would hear any piece of metal when it hit the copper tabletop. A consequence of stardom was that the world knew where to find you. The black stars of Hollywood had found all manner of letters from adoring folk, but they had also found straight razors and barbed needles nestled between parchments. Fingers had gone into envelopes and come out bloody.

Those without weapons made up for it with threats. Skip told me that he could spot a bad letter without opening it. A plump letter was a good one from a fan with lots to say. Hate mail was bone-thin. When we opened them, they always had big bold letters and language straight out of somebody's gutter.

The mail was brought home to conceal the ugliness of it. Word about threats and the like made Nat Cole look controversial, and the sponsors were skittish enough as it was. After Alabama, some venues didn't want him, because a man beaten onstage was an insurance liability.

One of the carriage house desks belonged to me and the other to Skip. His chair was rarely underneath it. Instead it was near one of the windows that filled the place with all-day light. It was as good as a watchtower, sitting on top of a three-car garage as it did. Between his walking rounds at night, Skip could stand in those windows and watch the property with clear sight lines to the Muirfield corner and the Fourth Street side.

The window carried that old handmade glass, full of ripples, like somebody had blown on it until it cooled. One pane was a new, machine-made replacement installed after someone had fired three bullets at the property a few years before. The first bullet shattered a guest room window in the main house, hitting glass a second time when it broke a mirror. A second ripped the wood paneling off the station wagon Nat and Maria took the girls to the beach in. A third broke the middle window of the carriage house.

Skip showed me where it had hit, and the bullet was still above our heads, deep in the crown molding. Wood putty hid the hole underneath the gloss of the trim paint. I wouldn't have known if Skip hadn't told me about it. It was our job to be mindful of such things, whether they'd been hidden or not.

Perhaps the one who burned NIGGER in the patch of lawn along Fourth Street was the same as the shooter, but most likely not. Walter told me he went out and turned the charred letters under with a spade and planted a camellia bush before the neighbors and gawkers passed. He worked hard on that yard, and every so often during our sort, Walter looked out the windows, looking for the trash people threw into the bushes and anything else that might be out of place.

"Yard looks good," I said. And he agreed. He wasn't one for false modesty, because he knew it was true as much as I did. Telling a yardman his work looked good was in some cases merciful, lifting his spirits while that sun beat him down. But calling the Cole grounds immaculate was gospel truth. It had to be the best yard on the block. If the people who gazed at the Coles' house, especially those who didn't want them around, looked hard for anything that was out of place, they'd be disappointed.

At the end of March, Walter had dug up a patch a foot deep and filled it with a truckload of limestone. On top of that he added gravel, crushed sand dollars, clamshells, and some bedrock the city had scooped out of the Los Angeles River after they'd dredged the bottom and poured down a new stretch of concrete. Walter finished the yard off with topsoil and a patch of grass as smooth as the living room carpet.

Walter missed a couple of mail sorts getting the yard

ready, but by April he was with us again, watching out the window while Nat practiced his short game. The putts he hit just then were breaking just right, and rattling the tin when they fell.

"Knocked two strokes off his handicap since January," Walter said. "Might be scratch by the fall."

Nat stood on his green with his golf coach, Jimmie DeVoe. They had called Jimmie the Jackie Robinson of golf, and he was teaching the Jackie Robinson of television. Everything had a Jackie then, but it stood to reason, because Jackie had won a Series and retired. It was hard being Jackie, though, and he had a head full of gray hair before he was forty.

After every round, they replayed the putts he had missed. He was meticulous about such things. Treat a detail like a small thing, and it'll get big in a hurry. Maybe that was what Jimmy was saying while he held the flagstick and looked at Nat's line to the cup, reading and reading. But all of his golf was with the sponsors, potential sponsors, so the score didn't matter as much as the deal that they never saw fit to make.

The mail table had taken on a new order, and the copper top was visible again. The stacks from the fans and well-wishers sat next to the signed photographs that would go back to them. We were finishing the last of it when Nat came up the stairs.

"You outdid yourself," Nat told Walter. "Jimmie says your little green is better than most."

"Might move the roses, get a load of sand and make a little bunker."

"You hear that, Lottie?" Elizabeth said. "Giving up roses for golf."

"Think Mrs. Cole might have a word to say about it first," Lottie said.

"I think her short game is better than mine, so she wouldn't mind one bit," Nat said.

Though the neat stack of the good mail was waiting for him, he passed it by and reached into the unsorted stack, and pulled one at random. The envelope that Nat opened and read was brightly colored with the deliberate letters of a child.

"There's a young girl in Cleveland who's lost a tooth, her first it seems. She doesn't love to smile like she once did, and school day pictures are coming."

He took one of the autographed pictures and added a note to the little girl in Cleveland. The 45 single of "Imagination" was coming out the next Tuesday, but we had a stack already. I would drop them in the air mail, so she'd get it before it came on the radio. Be the first in Cleveland to hear the brand-new song. Surely, snaggletooth and all, she couldn't help but smile like she used to.

Nat placed the girl's letter on the good stack and

reached for the other. After he read it, he returned it to the envelope and placed it on the pile. He didn't speak a word about what it said. He kept his hate mail a secret from the world, and he would take it all in, but he never showed it on his face. He couldn't afford to. Instead he wore the smile of a gambler, a smile that could mean anything or nothing at all.

"I need to know who I'm singing to. All of them."

With that smile he said good evening, and he was gone. It was about time for the rest of us to leave as well. I offered Lottie a ride home, but she said she'd work awhile. The Coles had put a television in the laundry room, and Lottie said she'd watch Dinah Shore while she folded the wash.

My landlords, Elizabeth and Walter, lived on the third floor of the Coles' house, so home was a short walk for them. Walter had lost his light for the day, so any yard work would wait until the morning. Elizabeth had dinner to fix for the Coles before her day was done. I saw them both standing over the little garden near the kitchen door, Walter with sheers and Elizabeth looking and pointing out the ripest peppers. He cut a few and a bit of the rosemary they stood in front of.

Skip had taken up his post in one of the wrought iron chairs, in the shadow of the carriage house and away from the light above the middle garage door. People had tried to get Nat to put up a fence or build a house way out of town. But part of being a star and staying a star was being seen. I had watched how people's faces changed when they saw him on the street. I couldn't imagine him hiding behind a gate. The Coles had done the opposite. A house on a corner with big windows, standing in the middle of everything where they could see and be seen. During the daylight hours the curtains were pulled back, because as Elizabeth and Walter might have said, the rooms needed daylight just like the lawn did.

Skip started his evening watch just a few feet away, and I finished my evening work, getting the car ready for the morning before I drove my own back across town to my place. Across the way in the main house, Elizabeth cooked dinner with the window open, and that rosemary was in a pot, and the smell of it had circled back through the open window and carried through the garden and toward the carriage house. No matter the past of sniper shots and angry neighbors, the Coles had made Hancock Park home, and we had been trusted to make sure that didn't change. The rest of the cohort looked out for the home front, and I made sure nothing came between him and his shows but the few miles of road we traveled to get there.

Chapter 24

It was a sure sign that she loved that job when Lucinda took me to Ivie's on her day off. The weekly specials on the chalkboard were in her handwriting. The dinner plate prices looked just like the phone number she'd given me at John Dolphin's place. That bit of leaning in her one. That lift in her eight, stretching up like an hourglass. Our waitress came to say hello, and so did half the others, giving me a good once-over to make sure I was decent enough for their friend.

Lucinda was dead set on me trying the chicken and waffles, a concoction that I had always found peculiar.

"I've seen people put cream and sugar on their grits. It can't be stranger than that," she said.

"The same kind of strange."

She pushed the plate across the table, parted the things between us—ketchup, butter, her coffee and mine—and offered me a portion cut and set aside. The table wasn't quite level, so the syrup had drifted toward the chicken, which was my main concern about having them on the same plate in the first place. Then I tasted a bite, and it all made sense for reasons I couldn't quite describe.

"I told you. I think the part of the brain that says 'delicious' is the same place that tells you something sounds good. That paprika and the maple syrup mixing together is like a nice little duet."

She pulled the plate back, and returned the coffees to where they had been. I offered her some of my eggs and chicken livers, but she said she was fine.

"This makes sense though, chicken livers and eggs pretty much started at the same exact place, so they go together," I said.

"No mystery on that plate. None whatsoever."

Ivie's was like all the Central Avenue breakfast spots that used to be more club than restaurant. Lucinda said it changed after Ivie died. That was around the time when Negro bands started to play the Sunset Strip. The old stage was demolished to make room for more booths, so the only music played now came from the jukeboxes. Each table had a small tabletop model, no bigger than those milkshake blenders behind the counter. The music came through the ceiling speakers between the air ducts and the ceiling fans, each song dropping along with the cool air and the light.

"Ivie was always sweet to me. She was touring with Duke until she got sick, but she'd saved enough money to open this spot. Gave singers jobs when we needed one. If one of us made a record, she'd keep it in the jukebox whether it hit or not."

Lucinda flipped through the pages of songs, some handwritten and some typed, their titles shortened to fit the space.

"Billy Strayhorn used to write songs at the counter. If Stray did something, everybody in town wanted to do the same. We kept pencils in our aprons so they could sit here and write. Ivie got tired of them using her menus for scratch paper, so she kept notebooks in the menu racks."

Everybody at the counter seemed too young to write a song. The counter jukeboxes fed the same speakers, so we heard what the young ears craved. That Los Angeles sound was something like a junction. Some Detroit and New Orleans, Memphis coming in. Some homegrown Angelenos.

When she found the page that listed her song, Lucinda paid a dime and dialed the number. 832. Before too long, it was our turn. I had thought I would have to pick her voice from a chorus, but she sang solo, a tune I had never heard about a city I had never seen.

When "Calhoun Street" came through the speakers, that swing of the horns started it off, and that piano came in, and she put space among the lyrics, playing a little hop-scotch with that easy Saint Louis stride.

"They had two train stations across the river in Memphis, on both ends of the same street. Last thing I saw before I left. Wrote a song and got myself a deal, not much but enough for me to know I needed to stay here."

That piano had a little Down South and a lot of Midwest in the chords, city around the edges and country at its heart. Lucinda took her time but she got someplace, patient but with one eye on the time. And then it was over, much too soon.

"Number nine on the Harlem Hit Parade chart. Top-ten record. My high point. Got to love your high point. Of course, I want to get a little higher next time, but still."

"Maybe I want to hear it again."

"The music goes around to every booth and the lunch counter, so everybody gets to hear their money's worth. Besides, I can't have my old song becoming your favorite, because you haven't heard the new ones. When I finish and record someplace. Seems like you're patient like me, Weary, so it'll be worth it when I'm done."

We started the afternoon with her work, and we finished with me doing mine. Driving. Though I spent my working days doing as much, I was fine carrying Lucinda anywhere she wanted to go. We took the road up to Griffith Observatory, and we could see everything while the sun came on down and covered Los Angeles in that early-evening light.

We got up to Griffith and found space along the over-look, where a guidepost on the railing listed the constella-tions. Proper stargazing required a trip up the mountain, because the streetlights did to the black sky what the smoky air did to the daylight blue. It was too early for stars, but that in-between color brought people out. The people who ended their daytime sightseeing left the place as the night crowd started to gather.

"I come up here quite a bit when Nat needs a little time at Capitol and I want to stay close."

"Nat Cole's a good man, getting you and Willie gigs like he did. Glad he stood up for you, considering."

"I guess Willie told you what happened."

"I knew about his jaw. And I'd heard about you even before he mentioned. I just didn't know your name. When I toured, I'd hear all kinds of stories on the bus, and who knows what's true. They used to talk about a soldier that jumped a stage. Some said Georgia and some Mississippi, but when I met Willie and Evelyn I heard it right. I had imagined what that fellow looked like. You're the spitting image of the man I pictured."

"You heard the rest of it. Kilby."

"I never heard that name, but just the way you say it, I know what that place is. I didn't want to ask. Why people come out here is heavy sometimes. They'll tell it when they want to. If they want to."

"Can't act like I'm ashamed. People might think I'm sorry for what I did. "

"You're here now though."

"Sometimes, but not always. Forgetting what you left is as much work as anything else."

"Stories I heard dwell on that fight, you being a hero and all, but they don't talk about the rest of it. They told me you were at that show with your girl. I imagine that takes some time to get over."

"That's why I came out here. Get some miles behind me."

"Takes time. When I got that call from Clora Bryant, that job, I was married. He begged me not to go on tour and told me he didn't know if he could wait. He told me Paris wasn't going anywhere. I said neither is the bottom, and I was tired of being there. If that's where I was meant to be I'd end up back there eventually. But that day I packed for Paris."

"I know you're glad you did."

"Just like I know you know you did right coming out here. That old feeling dies. Slow, but it goes. Plus I had a time over there. A few solos. Good choruses. That's my career, Weary. All that and a number nine record. Made enough money to put down on my house to make this home. You got to make it home, too."

Lucinda took a nickel from her pocketbook. I didn't intend for her to pay for anything but she was set on looking out at the city. While the telescopes inside were for nighttime viewing, the outside viewers were the day-time kind, and the dusk light was still enough to make it worthwhile. Five cents for five minutes so that we could see where we had already been and marvel at how small it seemed from the mountain. Lucinda kept one hand on the swivel and one on my shoulder, guiding me.

"You ever see Montgomery like this?"

"Got a little rooftop at the old hotel where our cabstand is. See a mile or two but not much to see."

The click of the telescope's timer got faster, that nick-el's worth of view running out as the eyepiece slammed closed. When it did, I dropped another coin, and the city was back for a little encore. Lucinda moved the lens.

"Take a look at Paramount."

A backdrop, a city skyline of New York or some likewise place, moved slowly along one of the back lot walls. For a moment I saw a little sliver of the red tractor that pulled it, with men out front directing the path.

"If we were on the other side of the mountain, I could pay to see NBC, and watch you and Nat driving onto the lot. Doing what we all come out here to do. Make shows and sing."

"Not for much longer, though. You know it's not going well. With the sponsors."

"People talk. Even if they didn't talk, I suspected as much. Watching the show and not a single commercial as good as that man is. I don't mind more singing, but I know how things work."

"I try not to dwell on it when he's around, but something good needs to happen soon."

"You need to be ready if things don't work. He's the most famous Negro out here. That puts him first in line for the good and the bad. I heard the station back home won't even show him. They'll dance to him, but they don't want to see his face."

Our viewfinder was still tilted toward the soundstages, but our change was gone. The sun was getting too low, and most of the valley was shadow-covered except for the lights that marked the streets.

"He steered clear of the nonsense, at least. Stepin Fetchit used to come into Ivie's sometimes, and he never wore the same suit twice. Nat Cole never cut the fool to make his money. I can say that, too. I've never sung anything I'm ashamed of. That's why Ivie hired us all, so we could pour coffee and make a living until a new gig worked out. If I never get another one, I never shamed myself trying."

"I still want to hear you sing again."

"I told you, once I get something down."

"No, I mean later this evening. Maybe in the morning. Maybe every so often. Whenever you feel like having me over to listen."

"I tell you what. Let me think about it while we drive."

And with that we were gone. Back down the mountain into the nighttime that was just then in the midst of falling.

Chapter 25

When I got my sister on the phone Marie had to raise her voice on account of the music, so she moved to another room. She asked someone to hang up the phone when she got there. Marie's voice came back, *I got it* and *thanks*, and that front room phone went back on its cradle, and half the party noise went quiet. That bedroom door creaked enough to hear her closing it, and the rest of the noise that had followed her down the hallway went quiet as well.

"So Dane tells me you met a woman out there. Happy to hear. Of course I wanted to hear in person, but it's good to hear your voice at least," Marie said.

"Every time I call it just rings and rings."

"We're careful about answering. The crank calls don't stop. People never set foot on a bus still mad we don't ride. Some of the nastiest gutter talk you'll ever hear. One said he'd kill me dead. I never understood why people say that.

Silly when you think about it. If they kill me, what else would I be besides dead?"

"Don't make light of it, though."

"Got to do something, otherwise we'll all go crazy."

"So that's why you're having a party on a Thursday night," I told her.

"It's a bail party."

"This connection must be bad, because—"

"Bail party. We're going to jail tomorrow, and by we I mean anybody who ran a carpool. Police want to round us up, but we decided we'd go early. Catch them by surprise before they come looking."

I wished she'd stayed in her party then, because the back room sounded lonely. Hearing her talk about Ripley Street jail in a quiet, empty place made it feel like she was already there. People were quick to say jail and prison were two different places, but that's a distinction folks make when they have never been to either.

"They just want to scare you," I said.

"They did, but we're all scared together."

I grew up hearing that steady line of her voice. I missed that dearly when she waivered, from bad news or grieving or tiredness. She was quiet for a little too long, but I didn't hear any crying. That breath, in and out, filled the receiver. Marie told me the walking wasn't the problem, and neither were the rides. It was the worry about what might come next.

"I think about that place, and I remember the last time I went. Couldn't even get close enough to see you when they took you," she said.

"Once you post bail you'll be in and out. Just like me, I'm out here."

"We're meeting at the Centennial lobby in the morning, so we'll be together at least. The women from the Council say we should call it progress. The city's losing money and the mayor's desperate. I'll try to call it progress, but I can't until I'm home."

"Like I said, in and out."

"We had a seminar the other night. What to do when you get booked. Taking a little tissue paper in our pockets. Leave our wedding rings and things at home. Strange, Nathaniel. In a Sunday school classroom studying how to go to jail."

"You'll be all right. Do what they told you, and you'll be out in a few hours. They'll drag it out, try to make you sweat, but you'll be fine."

She opened the door then, and that music came back in and kept her company.

"You're the disc jockey for our little set. The records came in the mail yesterday, so everybody told me to tell you hello and thank you."

"The new songs won't be out until Tuesday, so you all got a jump on folks."

"Good to be first, ain't it? You were there when he made them?"

"A couple. I got two by Nancy Wilson, because she has Dane's nose a little bit open."

"Yours, too, probably."

That bit of music just then was familiar, but it didn't come from the Capitol stack I'd sent to them.

"I heard that boy a few months ago. Dale Cook."

"That must be his brother or something, because this one's Sam. Whoever he is, they're about to wear out my needle, if the belt doesn't break first."

"I'll put some money in the mail. If I'm listening to your bail party records I might as well kick in. If I was there I'd buy some bourbon for the cause so you'd know I was committed."

"Committed means crazy."

"Nothing wrong with crazy as long as I have some company. Me and you can stay crazy together. Just be careful tomorrow."

"I will, love. Anyway somebody's about to take the phone from me. Itching to talk to you."

He took the seat that Marie left. That wood creaked along with that sigh of his. I heard my father before he said a word to me.

"How's the car running?" he said.

"Fine. So they got you in the middle of the bail party, too."

"Damndest thing I've ever seen. You know your brother's getting arrested, too. He's at the barbershop. They got a line out the door with folks going to jail tomorrow."

"Your son wants to look sharp for his mug shot. That's how it's supposed to be. Act like they're happy to be there, then nobody will get scared off."

"As of tomorrow all of my kids will have been down to that jail. I'm proud of every one of y'all. If you raise hell then we brought you up right."

Marie had switched out the old records to her new ones. An instrumental started then, and the lone voice was my father's baritone that he'd dropped to a whisper.

"E. D. Nixon pulled me aside the other week and told me he needed a favor. A big favor done in a hurry. Asked me to drive a fellow named Rustin out of town in the trunk of my car. You hear me? In my trunk. Not the taxi, my Sunday car. They said he's an organizer up north. Union man, he said. Me and Nixon go back, so I said yes. I figured we'd get a few miles out and I could let him out, put him in the front seat, but the fellow said no. Part of the discipline, he told me. The minute we relax and talk is the minute a trooper rolls up."

"That won't get you anywhere good."

"No, sir. We got to where he was going, and I opened the trunk. He shook my hand, said thank you, and he was in the wind. Would have liked to talk to him, you know, be hospitable. Told me he respected the courtesy, but it was a discipline thing. Can't argue with that, especially coming from a man ready to ride in the trunk of a car for that long. That's why I'm glad I took the Lincoln. If we couldn't have a decent conversation, at least I could give the man a little more room. The things that people have to do."

"You might as well be in it, if that's how you raised us."

"I know, but they told me I can't keep my pistol under my seat if I drive a carpool. Defeats the point of having a gun if you ain't carrying when folks act a fool. I'm not in charge, though. I'll leave it to your brother and sister and the rest. I can fix the ride cars and be good with that."

"That sounds like plenty."

"How's that car running?"

"I told you, it's fine."

"Just fine?"

"Better than fine. Wonderful."

"Your sister and Pete put some hours in that car before you came home. Me, too."

"And I appreciate you for it. Car's running pretty good, Pop."

"Just pretty good?"

"Better than good, then. I told you, Pop. It's fine. Quit your worrying."

"Like you don't."

"I'll take care of mine out here, and you look after everybody back home."

"I'll be out in front of Ripley Street when they make bail, don't worry."

It was for the better that they had a party, because they wouldn't sleep well. I lost sleep the night before I went to Ripley Street, but it wasn't on account of knowing what would happen. I had just figured wrong. I expected that day to change things, but I was dead wrong about how.

Chapter 26

Montgomery

DAY OF THE SHOW
4:3O P.M.

I had to take that ride out to Kilby. My father had told me to stop talking about that place, but I had made promises. I needed to keep it on my mind for a little while longer. After marching through Europe with Pritchett and George and Bone, I had promised them a show whether they were alive to see it or not. They weren't the only ones, though. I had also marched on the roads around Kilby Prison with more boys than I could name. If anybody needed a show it was them.

I remembered Nat's father at First Baptist. He ministered to the sick and shut-in, and on First Sunday afternoons he took communion to the homebound and ended his route with the folks in our neighborhood. He took his church on the road and brought them all a little taste of it like you might bring somebody a foil-covered plate of something still warm. I wanted to do the same for my Kilby gang, take them a little bit of that show they'd never get to see.

"I'm hoping you might take a little ride with me," I said. "I told some of the boys at Kilby I was going to work for you. Some believed me and some didn't. They been in there so long they don't know who you are. Never seen a television. All they know is that wall. I want to go show my face. I want them to see yours, too."

He nodded and got his coat and put that houndstooth on his head. With that we were gone to Kilby. I felt every mile of that drive as though the prison road were on top of me, pulled a little tighter across my gut the closer I got to the gate. It was a hard labor camp, and everything was work. Breathing was work. Keeping my mind right was work. So was calming the shake in my fingers on the steering wheel and the tremble of my foot on the gas. It was a fight. My body was asking why my mind saw fit to go back there.

Nat saw it for the first time.

"The one who attacked me. Was he out here?"

"He went to the cattle ranch. They got boys working a spread near the Mississippi line."

"How much time?"

"Three years."

"He's out in this world now, just like us."

The ranch was probably better work than Nat's attacker had ever had. I could hardly call the cattle ranch a prison. They were more cowboys than prisoners. I had heard about their steak dinners, and I hoped it was a lie, but envy will make a mind believe all manner of things. Children pretend they are cowboys, but I was yet to see any child pretend like he was on a road gang.

I drove slowly when I passed the first of the road crews stacking dead trees for burning. With so many gangs out, it was no telling who was who. I looked for the vertical stripes of the trusty, so I could find Polk. I had the window down, too, in case I heard him before I saw him. Three miles past the Kilby gate I caught his voice. The way he dragged out a holler told me it was Polk. Those work songs made me ill, and I didn't know a man who liked them. The only worthwhile reason to holler one was that I had some kindred to sing them with.

I pulled off the road slowly, and the two guards had already turned to watch my car. I got out carefully and took my time with my walk. Coming toward that first guard, I needed to let him know all was well. I carried a folded map in one hand, and the other hand was outstretched for a little friendly wave. I touched my hat.

A Kilby guard is a simple man. The curious type wouldn't work in a place like that, at least not for long. I answered their questions without saying a word, showed them what they already believed about me. I was a Negro driver of a long black car, looking for directions. The sun had found a seam, and it left a wall of glare on my windshield. The backseat was covered with shadow, so my passenger was unseen except for the one their simple minds put there. They surely thought I worked for a white man, and they would hesitate before messing with his driver. The longest ride they'd seen a Negro in was a paddy wagon or a hearse.

"Afternoon. My boss needs to get up to Wetumpka Road, and I got myself turned around."

I could tell the guard had been in the service. Most of them had. He was too young for my war, but maybe Korea. He wore his uniform sharp, as he'd been taught in the military. His new service as a Kilby guard didn't call for all that, and he'd learn in time. Before too long he would be as sloppy as his partner was, pocket flaps on his uniform curled up and wrinkled and his button line raggedy and an inch out of line with his belt buckle.

I bet he was a good shot, though. They all were.

The guard closest to me looked at my hands before my face, making sure he could see what I carried. The map was folded to the plot of land we stood on. In the same hand I carried a pack of cigarettes, an offering in exchange for his help.

"The new road ain't on this map. Turn around. Right at the fork up to Highway Nine."

He took two Kools, and then he took two more. He'd been in the Navy. The name of his ship was on the lighter he returned to his pocket as he breathed out the smoke.

"Menthol," he said and shook his head.

I got a good long look at the gang in the patch and saw three men I knew. Five were new boys in brand-new uniforms who must have come over from the boys' camp at Mount Meigs. They might have been sixteen if that and working their first Christmas on Kilby farm. A lot of boys thought about running that time of year. You were a fool if you didn't think about running and a bigger one if you tried.

The second guard carried his tobacco in his jaw, not a fistful like some of them chewed on, but a neat, tight bit he kept packing down with his tongue. I could trace his steps with his spit, gravel turned chaw-colored and the rocks mortared together in places with the juice and bits.

A small pine tree rested near the gravel's edge. The bottom cut was raggedy from the half-dull saws with too much tree sap and dust in the teeth. The guards would send a man after any midget pine tree, something to take home to his living room or sell for a dollar.

"You and your man got your directions. I guess y'all can get back on the road then," he said, handing the map back to me.

"Of course, I wouldn't leave without saying thank you and good afternoon, gentlemen."

One of the hardest jobs I ever had was smiling in a guard's face, but I needed to get close enough for the boys to be sure it was me. I'd come back like I told them, and somebody would tell it right.

God as my witness. I'd put my last dollar on it if I had a dollar left. Nat Weary was out on that road in a Packard with rock candy paint that was so smooth the dirt didn't have nowhere to grab hold.

The song Polk sang had a merciful time, slow enough for the boys to get a little rest without stopping. He leaned his shovel and kept the count, rocking that root loose on the downbeat. The year I'd been gone had passed over his face two- or threefold. The only clocks that moved quickly in Kilby were the ones that sped through our visiting time and the ones that aged us. Polk's crow's-feet were as deep as his scars. He squinted some, trying to see who I was.

The weather was cool at least, but December was too early for a freeze. The ground got stingy in the deepest part of winter, fighting a shovel, bending weak metal or a too-thin handle. But the dirt still had some give left. Still, watching them pull, I could feel the spread of my bones and the pull in my muscles, neither enough to get that root free.

Polk leaned into that shovel one more time and he

looked over at me, I nodded toward the car and he worked a chuckle into that song. He had never called me a liar, but I knew how it sounded when I told him before I left Kilby.

Got a job in California driving Nat Cole.

Got me a job, too. Joe Louis bought himself a jet plane, and he told me I could fly him.

Where to?

The moon first, and then on the way back we might stop in Cincinnati to see this girl I used to know. Get a bite to eat. A hot sandwich somewhere.

I'm not lying, though. That's where I'm going.

I know, Showstopper. That's why we gave you that name. Bring ol' Nat Cole by next time you come to town. Stop by the store and bring some cigarettes.

What kind?

Shit, man. The kind they sell at a store.

Once the guards turned away, I tossed the cigarette pack in the bit of tall grass just off the road. Polk saw, gave me that little nod we all gave in case the guards were watching, barely a nod at all. I couldn't give the boys a show, but they could smoke better. It was damn near Christmas, so a man could at least smoke some tobacco that didn't taste like the dirt it was pulled from.

The gravel under my shoes might have been the same rocks I had to carry in buckets way back when, and hearing the crush of them as I walked to the car was as bad as hearing those work songs. Nat by then had eased across the seat toward the near-side window. I told him to let the boys see him one good time. I figured that was as much show as we could give them. We sat for a moment before I started the engine, and Polk's work call got a little louder.

"This. Ten years of it," Nat said. He had learned to hide his anger just like we helped him hide that mail. People were used to that smooth croon when he opened his mouth. The other voice he kept away from the cameras and microphones. In the car, he didn't hide it.

"Ten years for giving that man what he had coming."

I nodded. "But I'm gone now. Last time I'll see the place."

I eased off the shoulder and onto the road, but I stopped by the guards so they could see who I carried. He stuck his head out of the window.

"I want to thank you, gentlemen," Nat said, looking at the guards but with his head tilted toward the men in that field. Lord, didn't his voice carry.

We drove about a quarter mile farther, and when the road widened I turned the car around, sending dust and rocks in a swirl behind us. Nat had his head turned to a group of boys near the shoulder. They looked like youngsters from the boys' camp cutting more pines for Christmas. The teenagers worked as trusties for the children who held armloads of pine branches for somebody's garland.

"All that time for a fight," he told me.

"Don't ever think I'm sorry for what I did. Your fingers. Your jaw. Your face. He would have smashed everything he could."

"I think about that night every time I get onstage. The ones who send the mail talk about it, say they'll get me again."

"They got to come for us first."

I drove a little faster then and turned up the radio, moving fast and thinking about the steps it took to cover the miles my gas foot pushed behind us.

"We never talked about it. How it felt when you put him on the ground."

"I guess I felt like you feel when you stand onstage. I understand why somebody wants that all the time. I'd do all I could to keep that feeling."

"That's the problem, Weary. I get that itch, and then I'm supposed to get humble, down-in-the-gutter humble, and forget they told me I was a star. I come off a stage with that fire running through me, and then I'm supposed to act like it's gone."

"To hell with it. Can't let anybody take that."

"They keep trying though, don't they? Not with a pipe, but they keep on."

"To hell with trying. It's the rest of it. What they do."

On the college station, George Worthy had started his

afternoon show with Nat's records, and the same secret that had been written across the Centennial's marquee was being told to anybody listening.

"My friends, the rumors you heard are true, tonight and tonight only . . . Montgomery's Very Own Nat King Cole. If you cannot make it to the Centennial then pull up a seat downstairs at the Majestic, or in your living room, because we will be broadcasting live. Get comfortable. Fix yourself a drink. We'll be playing nothing but Nat Cole from now until then."

When we passed my crew again, I wanted to give them a song. So I slowed down, let the engine dip just underneath the music so the boys heard a little something. No matter how slow I drove, they would get only a line or two of the record. We never got a whole song from a car passing on the road. A few bars. A hook maybe. The boys in the weed patch would make do with that much, just like those scraps of things they found on the roadside. A pop bottle turned into a still. A bit of metal from an undercarriage for a knife. A piece of copper wire to turn into a bootleg radio to catch some music when the wind and clouds favored us with a signal. If not, the men would piece together a story, make the show up from scratch.

We were out in the weed patch today and we saw Nat Cole riding in a Packard. I swear on the Bible Jesus carried that his driver was old Nat Weary.

Some days Nat wanted music on the car radio, and some days he didn't. I had always wondered how a singer who'd sold millions of records felt about hearing his own on the air. I imagine that it was a different kind of listening. I never asked him to explain. Besides, he didn't seem to hear it. He was turned all the way around looking out the back window then.

"The cigarettes you dropped. They'll find them?"

"Polk saw me. He'll get the word out."

"How many packs in the glove box?"

"Half dozen or so. I got a carton under the seat, too."

I gave him every pack, and when we'd rounded a corner, beyond sight of the road guards and the towers, Nat started throwing while his music played. The notes on the radio came from the hands that, thirty years before, threw curveballs, shot marbles, and skipped rocks. He was still a good shot, throwing menthol boxes along the prison road and finding the tallest clusters of chickweed where nobody would find what we'd left unless he knew to look.

"Do you remember that song, Weary? That last one they were singing."

"Yes."

"Who's Hannah?"

"She's the sun. They're asking her not to rise. That way it'll be over tomorrow."

"To sound like that in a place like this. I'd like to call it beautiful, but that's not the word. It stays with you, I imagine. Even when you don't want it to."

"Your people took you away from here so you'd never have to sing like that."

I prayed about those songs. If my mind went bad before the rest of me, I hoped those songs were the first things I forgot. My worn-out memory may show me mercy in the end. It would be nice to die believing I was never there.

Chapter 27

S CENE: Nat Cole driving a convertible down the Sunset Strip and singing "Anything Goes," in the brand-new MODEL from AUTOMAKER.

That was the number that Nat had created and that ad sales had pitched to a half-dozen potential sponsors. Nobody bought it. It was a good idea just the same, so they went ahead and produced it, because any good idea on the shelf would be worthless once the show was dead. So "Anything Goes" showed up on the rundown, the last song on the last episode of *The Nat King Cole Show.*

Innovation, Bob Henry said. They'd have to give Nat credit for that much. Bob and a cameraman had driven down Sunset Boulevard, shooting the clubs' marquees and their neon lights flashing in the evening. Nat would sit in a little Alfa Romeo convertible as that footage rolled across a screen behind him. The car came from the Warner Brothers lot, an after-hours favor from the property master in exchange for a few show tickets and some records. The show would end like it started, with homemade magic, some borrowing, and a good song.

I picked up the convertible from a lot filled with cars and anything else on wheels. I passed a covered wagon, a couple of chariots, a half-dozen police cars, and a Model A full of bullet holes that most likely belonged to some Hollywood gangsters. The convertibles, made for sunshine riding, were parked in a row under the west side fence. Nat had been specific about the make. For one, he needed a low windshield that wouldn't create much glare for the studio lights. The other reason wasn't spoken, but I knew for a fact that he didn't want to drive a car from a maker who'd said no to sponsoring him. Alfa Romeo didn't advertise on US television, so they'd never had a chance to turn him down.

While I drove the car onto the set, Mackie finished the Hollywood sign, with letters tall as the longboard he kept on his car. They arranged them just above the screen while I wiped the car clean. The first few letters looked plenty real hanging from the rafters. All of the HOLLY and the W had been lifted, and only the final three letters remained. Mackie carried an O above his head, and made a second trip for its twin. White lacquer covered the front of the letters, but the backs were unpainted and made from reused bits of plywood, some of them from the signs that welcomed the would-be sponsors, logos colored as bright as their store packages. No scraps of wood went to waste. They just started over as something else.

As the band started playing, the projector rolled on cue and did the moving for Nat. The song was about three minutes and the tape was four, long enough for Nat to say his good-nights and for the credits to roll. Four minutes was a short trip down Sunset, but Bob Henry had edited out much of it and spliced together the rest. He took out the no-name places, and let Ciro's rub shoulders with the Mocambo on the same block. His Palladium was a beat away from El Capitan. That Capitol Records steeple rose above the rooftops at the beginning and the end, and once or twice in the middle, so that Sunset looked more like a roundabout than a street.

As light and easy as that song was, that sadness in the room came from neither the lyrics nor the melody. The business made that number feel like an elegy. I had driven Nat to the Biltmore the night they gathered to tell him the show was canceled. The formality was meant to be a sign of respect, I imagine, but a steak dinner and a good scotch didn't make a dime's worth of difference to a man getting fired. They could call it what they wanted to, hiatus, cancellation. But they fired him. No other way to say it.

I held the door when he left the restaurant. He had that tall walk about him, but he was fallen just the same. His face didn't tell on him, because anytime I passed the Biltmore, I saw a couple of photographers, and their pictures ended up in the tabloids. That hotel was no place for a star to walk looking lost or broken. He had to look like who he was, a star whose name the magazines printed in bold letters.

Singing in the convertible with Sunset all around him, Nat headed toward the Biltmore once again. When Bob Henry did his cutting, the Biltmore's block was gone. Maybe it was mercy not to have it on the screen, or maybe it was just coincidence, and that slice of Sunset was as good as any to throw away.

With so much room between the microphone and the projector, the click of the film roll didn't rise above the music. I got an earful of it though, and it drowned out everything by the end of the song. The volume wasn't the problem. I was close enough to see that reel wind down, and three minutes and some change was all that was left of Nat's time on the air. After the song was finished, Nat had enough Sunset on the screen for the applause, his good-evening and thank-you, and the closing credits. Once that last bit of film snaked through the projector, it was over. Across Alameda Avenue, at NBC's color studio, the theme music and applause tracks for Robert Montgomery's show were playing just then, and any viewers still tuned to NBC watched him instead.

Nat raised his hands from the steering wheel as the studio audience applauded. He thanked them in that way that singers do, a makeshift bow with folded hands from the front seat of the roadster. I opened the door to let him out, and he gave them another bow then and a wave of the hand. Though the applause went on for some time, it had to end eventually, and the echoes followed close behind. And when that quiet settled in, the final episode had come and gone.

"Don't leave just yet," he told me.

The cargo door on the mountain side of the building was open, and between that corner of moonlight and the handful of clouds, the sky over the mountain glowed brighter than the studio.

"I'll drive," Nat said. "Get in."

During the show all Nat could do was pretend, so then he turned the key for real. The engine rumbled against the concrete floor, and he gunned it twice more before turning on the headlights and driving outside.

"Been ready to do this all day," he told me.

We took the back gate and turned into the Burbank traffic that had lightened by then. Nat hit the gas just enough to test that ride. Not the least bit of rattle or shake when we shifted and picked up speed. Just as smooth as it could be. The flip side of getting there in a hurry was that the ride ended too soon. Nat brought us the long way around Warner's until we reached the west entrance, where a property man waited for us. Merrill was cool enough about it, but I saw that bit of a double take he did when he saw who was driving.

"Thanks for the tickets," Merrill said.

"Did they take care of you?"

"Yes, sir, Mr. Cole. Never been that close to the stage."

I'd parked the Cadillac not too far from Merrill's desk, something huge and oak made, left over from a movie it looked like. It faced a television that had around it some makeshift rows of car seats and chairs from a multitude of times and places, captain's seats from boats and spaceships and shop-made benches built from scraps. Some of the stagehands must have watched with him. The television was still on, tuned to Robert Montgomery, who glowed in Technicolor, something brand-new for the top-money stars. The future of television, they called it, sharper colors and high-fidelity sound to match.

We got in the Cadillac and drove back toward the gate, but Nat stopped me before I could leave the lot.

"How about the once around? A few blocks of Los Angeles you haven't seen yet."

And so we circled the back lot cities and saw little bits of London and Rome and Manhattan on the same block. We made a few turns around the town square and its city hall at the top of the granite steps. The unnamed city was nowhere in particular, but who knew what it would be in the morning. Empty carriage bolts filled the space above the city hall sign, space enough to carry another name every time that town had cause to be someplace new.

"This is an amazing town when it wants to be," Nat said.

His voice was as steadfast as his poker face.

"The roadster was something else."

"It's not too late. I can work something out with Merrill. He likes the Crescendo. Get him a table and you can take the Alfa back out for a spin," I said.

"Some other time," Nat said, too tired to make it sound true.

Warner Brothers had those same tall backdrops that I'd seen inside the Paramount walls. At Warner's they let the newly painted canvases dry at night. Rows of them hung on the scaffolding outside Studio 27, all stretched out like so much laundry on the line. The one thing missing was the kind of wind that might sway them. And inside the studio doors, twenty feet of shelves carried the old cities, rolled up and stacked so they showed nothing but the little bit of horizon colors that bled onto the edges.

"I was hoping there'd still be time for good news," I said. "A few more shows through the spring at least."

"Good news takes time, and I don't have enough left. I told them to find me a sponsor, or end it. I paid as long as

I could, but I can't anymore. I almost lost my home once, and I can't ever go back to those days."

"In a year or two. Maybe they'll bring you back."

I knew good and well what the answer was before he said it.

"It's dead, Weary. They don't bring us back."

I didn't say anything. We had gone through all the "look on the bright side" talking. The contingencies and possibilities had come and gone.

"The last time a show died on me was back in Montgomery," he said. "I've been thinking about that more than I've let on. Maybe I should go back. At least I can say the last time I was down there I gave the folks a show."

I didn't know what to say at first, because I didn't think I was ready to go back there. Los Angeles and my work and his show were meant to be my cure. But when Nat mentioned going home, it seemed then that my ailment was the same as his. Of all the shows he had done, that one he'd never forgotten. We'd always be tied to it, the back side of an interruption, trying to get back in front.

"Nothing's changed down there," I told him. "If anything, Montgomery's worse. The way they're acting with these busses, somebody's liable to kill you."

"The ones who didn't want me to finish my show got what they wanted," he said. "But now. Seems my schedule is about to open up. I'll be damned if they stop me again."

His voice had a little more fire in it then, and the embers spread like fires do, with me close enough to catch some. Show business people know how to turn their anger into a song. A show. Maybe I'd learn to do the same thing I'd seen him do on live television. Change that burning into starlight.

"With that camera, I never know who I'm singing to. Judging by the mail I have plenty watching who didn't want me to finish. Whether they want me to or not, I stare them in the face and sing. I learned that a long time ago, but I learned it in spades at the Empire. You help me set up a show, and I'll try it again in Montgomery."

"Whatever you need me to do."

"Good. Give the homefolk the show they never got to see," he said. "You, too, friend."

It had started then as a make-believe notion passed from him to me. Then it became something possible, and beyond that something that was necessary. I saw it, and heard it, repeating in my head. From there, it was just a matter of making it so.

Chapter 28

Montgomery

DAY OF THE SHOW
5:30 P.M.

Pete had my car on the lift to change the oil and get me set for my travels that next morning. He talked about my Packard like it was his, and for a good long while it had been. He worked on all the cabs, which together had probably driven a million miles around Montgomery, but those were circles. Mine was the first car of his that had made a round trip through the desert and was set to go back to California. He looked for something wrong and admired his work at the same time.

"Salt," he said. "That's where most of the problems start, but not that salt in the water and the air, I'm talking 'bout the road salt up north. It eats through the bottom like nothing. Out west it's sand, see, it gets in the block and starts trouble. Your oil is old, but it ain't too filthy. Car like this, you can drive it forever if you keep it up."

He stared at the undercarriage, going back and forth with that light he held.

"You got a good mechanic out there?"

"You know I do my own work."

"Your stingy ass makes good money, so you need a real mechanic."

"Who says I'm not one?"

"I'm saying it to your face. Just because you drive a car don't mean you can fix one. Eating ham ain't the same as raising a pig."

Marie came out of the station with a handful of candy, some cinnamon and some honey. She split it with me.

"What's Pete talking about?"

"Nothing but some trash."

"Nathaniel was telling me how much he'll miss my work tomorrow when he's gone," Pete said.

"Hell, I might miss you, too," I said.

"Don't understand the rush," Marie told me. We stood near my front fender. She wiped the cinnamon dust from her hands before she reached up to the tire and measured the tread with her fingertip.

"Been here a good solid week," I said.

"You talk like that's any kind of time."

The boycott had taken its toll. Marie and Pete kept the

pumps locked at night so they couldn't be firebombed with their own gasoline. The shattered front window had been replaced once, and in case another brick was thrown, the plywood stood at the ready behind a stack of radial tires. Crossed strips of electrical tape covered the new window and the garage door glass. In case the panes were broken, the brick wouldn't make it through and hurt anyone. With all the busted windows, the boycott year had done to Montgomery what hurricane season did to the Gulf. The difference was, storms didn't choose. They just rained on everybody.

Marie and Pete's carpool ran on odd-numbered days and every other weekend. The stops moved around for safety. The organizers moved, too. The Montgomery Improvement Association and the Women's Political Council never stayed in the same space more than a few days at a time. I had passed the sewing space over the dry cleaners and wondered if Mattie still ran her newsletter out of there. I wanted to speak to her before I left.

When I asked Marie where I could find Mattie, she didn't say anything at first. She checked the tire's tread again.

"It would be strange for me not to say something. Been here all this time. It might seem rude."

Marie didn't answer. She had moved on from the tire, messing with a sprig of pecan leaves caught under the fender.

"Plus, I want her to know about the show. She and her husband are welcome."

She hadn't answered me yet.

"She still moves the office around?"

She nodded, hesitated, but then she went ahead with it.

"She's at Gray's today. The repair shop around back. Mr. Gray fixes the print machines, so they work there some days."

Marie told me she'd drive my car to make sure the tires and the brakes were fine. Before she took the keys, she squeezed her words into my palms.

"That's the problem with coming back. You start to dwell."

"Just a good-bye, and then I'm gone."

She let go, then clutched my keys like she meant to pray for them.

"We'll have your car ready when you get back."

The bell of the repair shop rang when the door opened, and I couldn't see anybody. The shelves carried the hulls of radios and the insides of turntables. A few televisions had been cracked open, ready for the new tubes stacked on the shelves. It was the perfect back room for that boycott office, because the wall of radios hid Mattie from anyone walking in. I saw her hands through an open space. She cleaned them with a can of hair spray and wiped the ink away with a piece of terry cloth. The shop was small, so the smell of the aerosol, powder, and oil filled the place, as the mist crossed through the circle of lamplight.

"Yes? Hello?"

"Mattie, it's me."

We didn't touch this time. The smile across the room was respectable.

"I asked Marie about you, and she said I could find you here. I was in town for a few days, but I'm leaving tomorrow. I wanted to speak before I did."

"I saw your car at the hotel, so I thought you might be here for a visit."

"Not just visiting. Nat Cole's here. We have a show this evening down the street. The old stomp."

"I heard some talk earlier this afternoon. Nice when a good rumor turns out to be true. I suppose we can all thank you for bringing him."

"We wanted to bring folks a show. Just needed to keep it quiet this time until the last minute, but I wanted you and Oswald to know about it. Plenty of good seats so we want people to know."

"We appreciate you," she said.

I had to remind myself to keep talking, because the quiet was only good for staring and hearing things said so long ago. Things that needed to be left where they'd fallen. She had crossed her arms in that way she used to sometimes, with that ring finger making circles round and round her elbow.

"I hear it might be over soon. The busses. Good news for you all," I said.

She crossed her fingers, but I knew she didn't put much faith in luck. It was just something else to do with her hands. Mine were in my pockets.

"Waiting to hear back from the Supreme Court, if you can believe it."

"I believe it, Mattie. Your work got you somewhere. Maybe you can celebrate when it's over."

"More relieved than anything else. For a while at least. There'll be something else after this though. Schools. People want to vote. I guess we're ready for all of that now."

"You always have been."

Of all my plans and wondering about Nat's show, I had to wonder about my unfinished business in Montgomery. It was my hope that we could both move on with no more questions. We were testing the bit of peace we'd made, to see if it was good and settled.

After I moved to Los Angeles, I wondered about seeing Mattie again. If I would. When. How it would be. Maybe a benign reunion of old friends, with enough of my new life around me to kill all the old craving. But it was anything but that. The boycott, planned at first for just a day to send a message, had lasted through the winter and the spring, and Montgomery had made all kinds of news. Mrs. Lomax's stories in the *Tribune* brought Montgomery to Los Angeles, not just on the pages but in person.

A June headline announced a rally in support of the boycott at the Dunbar Hotel, and posters lined the shop windows on Central Avenue, listing speakers from the Women's Political Council and the Montgomery Improvement Association, among them Mrs. Mattie Green Allen. With every seat filled, a couple hundred easily, I watched from the standing room outside the mezzanine's doors.

Mattie talked about struggling, but struggling on the way to something and someplace. *The patience of Negroes has been abused.* Waiting, she told them, was moving backward while the world slipped ahead. *Six months of walking has moved us, the Negroes of Montgomery, ahead by years, but it's hardly far enough. We still haven't reached a moment of equal treatment.* It seemed that Los Angeles was filled with folks who'd left Montgomery, but they had called theirs different names. Galveston. Baton Rouge. Jackson. Little Rock.

Mattie's voice had for so long been familiar to me, but in that ballroom it was electric. I might have lied to myself and believed I wanted only to speak to her. Maybe I could say I just went to show my face and say a respectable hello, but I wanted more than that. I wanted to say what was still on my mind. When the speeches and the handshaking were over, I called up to her room on the house phone. I needed to talk at the very least. When I asked if she would see me, she said yes.

We had been married once. Just two names on the register at an Oklahoma hotel. So there we were again. A fine room in Los Angeles with no name on the register. We didn't have to write down the lie or say it out loud to anyone.

"They sent you to fight, Nathaniel. And Kilby. The people who sent you never felt any shame for how they did you. I don't believe in being ashamed, Nathaniel. Judged by people who took everything."

I wondered about the other life, getting married in the Kilby church and making children on a prison mattress, having some time with my wife in a room with no door and no curtains. Maybe, if I was good and did what the guards told me, I could hug my children's necks on Christmas. Mattie and I had traded that life for separate ones, except for that night in a Dunbar Hotel room. We squeezed out the last bit of that feeling, and maybe that was what I needed to get myself right.

"I want you to have as good a life out here as I have at home. The one I'm going back to. None of that has any-

thing to do with you and me right now. This is all we have."
That's what she'd told me.

We let good-bye become a feeling, the last promise we
could make to one another when we got through. I had
to put that feeling down and leave it all there, let it rest.
When daylight came, she was on the Sunset Limited and
I'd left for home, getting to my porch just after the morning paper. The front-page news was about the charge Mrs.
Allen left. *We have lived too long with the lopsided portions,
always the last and always the bottom. Lay down the pieces of
that life and make the one meant for us, with all of the honor
and none of the shame.*

So back in Montgomery, standing there with Mattie in
the hidden office, the workshop of the small things that
needed tending and backroom plans, we said good-bye
and thank you without another word. We'd already run
through the last of them, and they didn't need repeating.
When she turned around she got her machines going
once again. The last of me in that place was the sound of
the silver door chimes, that quick bit of rustling that told
Mattie I was gone.

Chapter 29

On that last Sunday afternoon before leaving for Montgomery, I sat with Lucinda on that narrow porch, cozy she called it, with just enough room for her gunmetal love seat. She sat with her feet in my lap, rolling her heels one way and flexing her toes the other. She had once told me about the dance steps her chorus did. Her feet told the same story, ankles rolling around and around.

"I'm going home for a little while."

"I have to get ready for work soon anyway," she said and poured some of that tea she made in the sunlight, setting it on the porch wall to let it sweeten.

"No. I mean Montgomery."

"Everybody all right?"

As light as that day was supposed to feel, that bit I had not told her weighed on me. I knew it would get heavier until I told it.

"Nat had an idea. Well, we both did. He wants to put on

a show back home. Give the folks the one he didn't finish.
I'll be gone for a few weeks."

She didn't say much for a minute. Just a little turn in the
winding of her feet.

"Back to Alabama, then."

"Just for a couple of weeks."

She lifted her hand to my shoulder and sat up, and her
feet stopped their leaping as she set them on the ground.

"And then what?"

"Nat might be gone for a while, but plenty of folks need
drivers. I'll figure something out when I come back from
home."

When she lifted off the seat, the bench rocked, and the
creak of the spring counted the back and forth I did there
sitting alone, while Lucinda stood on the edge of the patio.

"You keep calling it home, Weary."

I wished what she said wasn't true. My yearning had
done me harm on occasion, taking my mind to old places.
But I followed and let it be. On that evening in June when
I left Mattie's hotel room, the quickest ride home would
have taken me right by Ivie's. Instead of driving along Central, I took the long way around. That guilt took me blocks
out of my way, because some mornings Lucinda worked
the midnight shift that stretched until after sunrise and
she might wonder why I would pass without stopping at
that hour of the morning. I was not a man with lies at the

ready, and I didn't want to get caught trying. I had done
that bit of backsliding, but I had put most of that old-time
yearning behind me.

"When are you leaving?"

"Before the week is out."

My leg had fallen asleep while hers were on top of mine.
And as the nerves came awake again, tingling and fire, I
wondered if dreaming happened in the muscle and skin. I
stayed on that seat, because I couldn't stand up and trust
my steps. It would be hard to walk with one leg slumber-
ing and the other wide awake.

The back porch shared a window with Lucinda's bedroom, and the view was the same one we saw at night, listening to her songs when we made time. While the record
spun she hummed along, on my chest and in my ear, and
turned her live voice into a duet with the one on vinyl.
Lucinda counted time on my skin, with a knee across my
thigh, fingers on breastbone. I had hoped that morning
might take its time getting there, stay back east for a while
longer so we could fit in a few more hours of night. Sometimes on the patio she opened a window so the music that
filled the house could join us outside. But on that afternoon, there was nothing but outside noise and the love
seat's creaking, which went away when I stopped it from
swinging.

"Your friend, the woman from the theater—"

She didn't ask a question, but I felt it there just as sure as the concrete under my feet.

"She's married."

"So was I. Doesn't make you stop wondering."

"That was a long time ago."

"The years don't matter as much as how they feel to you. You can hold on to a time and keep it close. Too close."

She did not ask me if I had seen Mattie, but if she did I would have lied. I might have told the front end of it, hearing that speech down at the Dunbar. But the rest wouldn't have done either of us any good. Lucinda told me I didn't know where I was yet, home or someplace else. I was still in the middle of getting right, so I could tell only as much truth as I was certain of.

"I'm going back to put on the show, and then I'm coming back."

"I hope it looks different to you. Feels different. If it doesn't there's not much reason to come back at all. Guess you won't know until you get there."

She had a question in the middle of what she told me, but I could only answer with speculation. The sooner I got down to Montgomery, the sooner I would know for sure.

Chapter 30

Montgomery

DAY OF THE SHOW
6:10 P.M.

You all right, Mr. Weary?"

I had not yet seen her in Montgomery, but Mrs. Lomax was there waiting when I got back to the Centennial, sitting with her Dictaphone in a case at her feet.

"Look like you might have gotten a little winded," she said. Saying good-bye to Mattie had tugged at me for a good long while, so I'd walked with it down the block and back, carrying that feeling. It still had some weight to it, so carrying that up the steps might have left me looking spent.

"I believe I'm fine. Or I will be soon. I had a list of things to get done before the show. Making sure I leave here with no worries. I'm a little run-down, but I'll be better."

"Don't worry. I covered most of the musicians on Central Avenue; promoters, too. The nerves go away when the show starts. And by the look of that line outside, you did just fine. Of course, I can't forgive you for keeping this a secret, but I think the consolation works just fine."

I had promised Mrs. Lomax an interview. True to her word, she was staying in Montgomery until the boycott was over, and we still weren't there yet. She had been gone, but I'd kept up with her on her news pages. Before she had left Los Angeles, she had written about Jim Crow in Hollywood like it was the City Lines bus, and she had written up the boycotters like they were superstars. In her next paper, she could write about both.

"Glad he agreed," she said. "Candor can be hard in Mr. Cole's business. For some of them the show never really stops. They can never turn it off long enough to tell me what I need to hear."

"When he's got something on his mind, he's careful about who he tells. Now seems like the right time. He wants to talk about what happened to the television show."

"Hiatus," she said.

I shook my head. "They've kept it quiet. Say he's touring, but he'll tell you the whole of it."

"You were right to call me then, Mr. Weary. I'm the one to talk to. I have a dozen papers that'll pick up the interview in the morning."

She handed me a business card, Lomax Wire Service.

"We're looking for a buyer for the *Tribune*. I could either be there to run it, or I can be here. It was a hard call, but I have to stay. Three Negro papers in Los Angeles, and soon there'll be two. There's exactly one Negro news service in this city, and it's mine."

"Have to start over sometimes," I told her. "We both know that now."

"Being new here let me tell it right. Reporters from the white papers have been in and out, but they come for a few days or a week maybe. I couldn't cover it like that. I needed to be here to understand."

She walked to the window and pointed toward the Dexter parsonage just down the block. The house had been repaired, but it was easy enough to see the damage. The new shingles were the same color as the old, but years of fading had given them a color hard to match. So the line was easy to see. The street light bounced differently when it hit the old tiles and the new.

"I was here before they bombed it, so I saw that hole in the nursery wall. I sat in there with Mrs. King not a week before. It feels different when you know a place before the next round of trouble starts. This city is the same."

I had passed the parsonage enough times to know the swing was gone. Anything there when the bomb exploded—slats, carriage bolts, and the chains—would have been as deadly as a bullet if they'd hit the Kings. The worst kind of blast makes shrapnel of the simple, comfortable things. Mailboxes. Rocking chairs.

"I met the preacher before I left here. Sad that his house had to burn to make a name for himself," I said.

The gardens at Saint Margaret's Hospital ran the length of the block along Jackson Street. It stood to reason that sick folks or their families might find a little bit of comfort looking at the flower beds and birdbaths, but I wondered what they thought, minds troubled or bodies ailing, the night they looked out the window and saw a parsonage burning.

"The hero business is a strange one," Mrs. Lomax told me. "For every name I see somewhere, I talk to a dozen people who have to hide their work for all kinds of reasons. People I admire all have a little dirt on their shoes. Like you."

"I'm an ex-con. So I got plenty dirt on mine."

"I worked for a newspaper owned by a racketeer, one who bought a hotel and named it after Paul Laurence Dunbar. A so-called gangster with an ear for poetry. We're complex folks. It takes more than the saints to handle trouble."

She rose then, because Skip was in front of Nat's room with the door a bit cracked. He was close to being ready for her. Skip held up his fingers and signaled that she could come on down in a few minutes. I had one more question before she left.

"This might sound strange, but I need to know. Have you asked anybody about me? I mean, I know people tell that story and have a little bit of fun with it, but what do they say when my name comes up?"

"They're sorry about what happened to you."

"Sorry."

She nodded yes.

"I came back so that won't happen again. This time tomorrow when they hear my name, they'll be talking about the show. Let that be my high point, and then I'll be gone on home."

"I understand, Mr. Weary. Leave something behind you besides dust. Still, though. I heard you beat a man with a microphone. And in my work, I've beaten a few myself. It's a good feeling, isn't it?"

All I could say was yes.

"So long, Mr. Weary."

Mrs. Lomax picked up her Dictaphone and headed down the hallway. Skip tipped his hat and let her into the room. What she recorded I could only speculate on. It wasn't my business to ask Nat. The back of her card listed the papers that carried her news wires, and I would pass through a few of those places on my way west. I'd find myself a newspaper. Nat had been so quiet and so careful, and he no longer had to be.

Chapter 31

Montgomery

DAY OF THE SHOW
7:45 P.M.

The doors opened fifteen minutes ago, at seven thirty.
When the time came, I went upstairs to watch the
crowd enter and get their first look at the stage. The bandstand's colors warmed the place, and the new wax on the
hardwood spread the colors all over the floor. The elevator
and the front stairs brought the crowd up from the lobby,
filling the banquettes along the side. Their voices filled
the place as well. In the studio, everyone was so careful
of the least little sound that might kill a song, but on a live
record the sounds let you know that music had been someplace, made in a room full of good times and laughter.

The New Collegians would start the show with "Tuxedo
Junction" until Nat came up the stairs and took the stage.

The crowd would roar then, and with the transoms open, that sound would make it down the side of the building. Maybe some of the music would get into the copper rainspouts and spiral down to the sidewalk.

I walked up and down the back staircase to make sure no one lingered. Skip had done the same with the front. Miss Vee and her people watched out for the front door, and Dane watched the back near the cabstand. The mob of folks who came for Nat last time would have nowhere to hide in the Centennial. So a locked door and a watchful eye would keep the show safe from interruptions. With that, all we needed was the music.

When the interview was over, and Mrs. Lomax had taken her seat in the ballroom, I went back down to sit with Nat like we did on television days, telling him something or just letting him tell me whatever he had on his mind.

He pointed to the ceiling.

"Listen to your room, Weary."

The foot tapping worked through the brick and joists, the lathe and the plaster. The New Collegians changed players every year and mixed in some new sounds with the old, but the fanfares were staples, so the sound I anticipated came to me note for note.

"I want to tell the folks a little story about Saint John

Street and how I got my name. I want to make sure I get it right."

"Any way you tell it will be fine."

"They've been patient for all these years, friend. You along with them. I'll give them what they came for."

The clapping came in time with the fanfare.

"I need to thank you for bringing me back."

"No you don't. All you have to do is give them a show. We do it right, then they'll talk about it for years."

The knock on the door meant five minutes from show-time, and with that I walked Nat up the back stairs and to the steel door at the side of the stage. My chair sat in a corner to the left of the bandstand. And I took my seat before the spotlight came on. The audience got their first view of Nat Cole.

Then came the sound that everyone should hear at least once, the roar of strangers cheering just because you showed your face. Nat thanked them and took a few min-utes to say hello, and to introduce the New Collegians one more time. He was also giving Willie and Evelyn time. It was a smooth and unnoticed way to get the sound just so, because sound check or not, when a room fills, so many things change. Evelyn worked the levels, and Willie was on the reels.

Nat started with a familiar question.

In the evenings, may I come and sing to you?

Someone shouted yes.

All the songs that I would like to bring to you?

And then it started. Willie checked the reels one more time. They moved like the first slow turns of train wheels, at the speed of anticipation. Three shows started all at once. The live show for the ones in the room. The live show on the radio. The show on the reels for future listening, the tomorrow show for all who would listen in the days that would arrive in time.

And I considered the time between now and back then, the long-ago show that he never finished, and Nat standing there bruised singing "I've Got the World on a String." He'd put that first on the set list. The years notwithstanding, he would pick up right where he left off.

I watched two shows of Nat's come to an end, one because of money and the other because of a man with a pipe. I prepared for both. As for men with pipes or anyone else, I placed my chair near the side of the stage, out of sight.

I had reached the place where I looked forward more than back. I looked forward to the horn solos, the long, held notes. I always marveled at the kind of breathing going on underneath, the laboring hidden under a single sound. Instead of something cobbled together, the sound was woven tight like gabardine, so all to be heard was the one thing and not the pieces.

Evelyn and Willie collected every note. Echoes had stopped chasing the sound. Maybe they'd decided to sit back and listen, or perhaps, instead of bouncing and mocking, they sang along in time.

I watched people listening, wrapped in the right-now sound spinning all around us like it did on turntables and in that wind that carried the tide of radio waves. The sound pushed back the outside noise from the streets below, the rattle and whine of the emptiest busses. The people who came that evening had enjoyed either a walk or a ride to get from home to their seats. And the lights had gone low, except for the ones meant for the stage. I needed to see it, that look on their faces when that moment began. The waiting was behind them, because we had brought our people the show they had imagined for so very long.

Acknowledgments

I am thankful for the generous support of the National Endowment for the Arts, the Hemingway Foundation, PEN New England, Ucross Foundation, Bread Loaf Writers' Conference, and the Baton Rouge Area Foundation for funding and residencies that helped me to complete this novel.

Thank you to the staff of the Rosa Parks Museum and the Davis Theatre for the Performing Arts for tours and notes on Montgomery history. Both facilities are entities of Troy University Montgomery, an important center of downtown preservation.

I also appreciate the efforts of Alabama State University and those involved in the salvage and restoration of Nat King Cole's childhood home. I am likewise grateful for the work of Mr. Edward Davis, owner of the Ben Moore Hotel, who granted me access to the facility and answered questions about Centennial Hill and Montgomery in the 1950s.

I appreciate the work of the Paley Center for the Media, locations in New York and Los Angeles, where hours of Nat King Cole footage are available for public view and research.

Thank you to the staff of the Emory University Manuscript, Archives, and Rare Book Library. The collected papers of Almena Lomax provided deeply engaging insight into her work chronicling the civil rights movement.

I have shared this work with my fellow *Callaloo* Creative Writing Workshop faculty, Maaza Mengiste, Gregory Pardlo, and Vievee Francis. Thanks to them and to *Callaloo* editor Dr. Charles Rowell for generous feedback, support, and encouragement.

I am indebted to Sanderia Smith and Nelly Rosario for their generous notes on the novel. I also appreciate the good counsel of Dr. Kern Jackson and our conversations on Albert Murray and the Alabama blues aesthetic.

I am likewise grateful for the support of Marita Golden and the Hurston/Wright workshops for helping me to shape my voice. I continue to cherish the instruction I received at Howard University and the MFA program in creative writing at the University of Virginia.

As always, I thank my wife, Laura, and our boys, Ellis and Cole, for their love, support, and patience. Thanks to my mother, Caroline Yelding; my father, Leon Howard;

my sister, R. Jai Gillum; and my brother-in-law, Andrew Gillum.

I am, as always, thankful for the support and good counsel of my editor, Claire Wachtel, and my agent, Dorian Karchmar, whose advocacy and feedback have supported and enhanced my journey through publishing.

I am thankful to so many in my hometown, Montgomery, Alabama. Most of those who made the bus boycott successful did not become famous, but they shared their stories with younger generations. As a youngster I met some of the activists, and I surely crossed paths with the anonymous many.

We can never know or call every name, but we can show them the work made possible by their efforts, sacrifices, and triumphs.

About the author

About the book

Insights,
Interviews
& More . . .

Meet Ravi Howard

Author photograph by Bert Irving

RAVI HOWARD won the 2008 Ernest J. Gaines Award for Literary Excellence for his novel *Like Trees, Walking*. He was also a finalist for the Hemingway Foundation/PEN Award. Howard has received fellowships and awards from the National Endowment for the Arts, Hurston/Wright Foundation, Bread Loaf Writers' Conference, and the New Jersey Council on the Arts. Howard's work has appeared in *Callaloo,* the *Massachusetts Review,* the *New York Times,* and on NPR's *All Things Considered.* As a sports producer with NFL Films, he won an Emmy in 2005 for his work on *Inside the NFL.* He lives in Atlanta, Georgia. ∾

A Q&A with Ravi Howard and Tayari Jones, from *Salon*

Ravi Howard talks about Nat King Cole, the South, and when it's OK to take liberties with history.

(This Q&A first appeared on *Salon*. Reprinted courtesy of *Salon*.)

Tayari Jones: *So first off, how is the weather down there?*

Ravi Howard: I almost hate to say it to people who are not down here, but we got into the sixties today.

TJ: *Don't rub it in. I'm wearing my puffy coat indoors at this point.*

RH: I'm not rubbing it in. I feel your pain. You remember that I lived in New Jersey for seven years.

TJ: *Did you write much when you were up here?*

RH: When I was up there I was writing about Alabama, but I was writing about the South from a remembered space. Even though I had been gone for years, stories about home were primarily what I was writing and imagining.

TJ: *Same here. Even though I have mastered the New York subways (at* ▶

last), when I sit down to write, my imagination unfolds in Atlanta. This is why I will always think of myself as a Southern writer, no matter where I happen to hang my hat.

RH: Didn't I just see that you were invited to join the Fellowship of Southern Writers?

TJ: *Yes! I am so excited. Often, I am not considered a Southern writer, because I am black and writing about Atlanta and urban spaces. So I wanted to be let into the Southern writer party.*

RH: Yes, it's important that black writers claim and be claimed by the South.

TJ: *So I'll take that to mean that you think of yourself as a quote-unquote capital S Southern writer?*

RH: Yes, but I prefer the idea of layers of labeling. We can define ourselves with those layers. Black writer. Southern writer. Some folks are Urban Southern. Historical Southern. Gulf Coastal writers. Layers give you specificity. And you can use as many layers as you need to get to the heart of the matter.

Driving the King is my second novel set in Alabama, and that specificity is important because it lets me return to that space because I can fine-tune the characters and space without the feeling of being pigeonholed.

TJ: *What if you are a pigeon and that's your hole? I kind of feel like that sometimes.*

RH: (laughs)

TJ: *Alabama is the second most Southern state, in my view, just after Mississippi. Did you see* Selma? *I loved how it was completely Alabama and completely Southern, and completely dignified. A lot of spray starch was expended in the making of that film!*

RH: I'm excited to see it, and I'm going this weekend. I saw a *Selma* presentation by Ava DuVernay at the Bronze Lens Film Festival. I loved her first two films.

TJ: *One thing I thought about* Selma, *and it made me think of* Driving the King, *is the way that a certain African American middle-class affect performance was still a part of the movement.*

RH: As a writing exercise for my students, I give them pictures of James Hood and Vivian Malone on the day they integrated the University of Alabama. They're surrounded by press and police. You can look at his hat, and you can look at her dress and tell that they had gone through certain motions preparing, almost this sense of character development for that moment. It speaks to what we do as writers, ▶

showing what happens before people get on that fiction stage. *In Driving the King*, we have Nat King Cole, a black star, his chauffeur and his car—they are an extension of that. As he's moving from one stage to the next, there is a sense that he must always be prepared for the next moment. I wanted to show the parallels between black Hollywood and the civil rights movement. There was a sense of casting there. Jackie Robinson. Martin Luther King Jr. Rosa Parks. None of them were the first to try and do what they did, but they were perfectly cast at the right time. Same with Nat King Cole. He wasn't the first singer, but he was the right man at the right time.

TJ: *How did Nat King Cole become Nat King Cole? I think that's the question of your novel, right? There are two boys, both named Nathaniel, both black in Montgomery. Where one become known as "King" and the other by his last name, "Weary."*

RH: Nat King Cole was a great piano player in a trio, and then it became obvious that he was a great singer. He needed to be in the same space as Sinatra and the other great singers at the front of the stage. I think he embraced that, hoping it could break open doors for others who wanted television shows.

Also, he and Jackie Robinson were good friends and would watch each other. So I think that friendship was a result of that role. Prime-time television was Major League Baseball. He referred to himself as the Jackie Robinson of television at one point. Black entertainers recognized the history they needed to make.

TJ: *Speaking of "making" history. This is a historical novel, but you took a lot of liberties with the record, didn't you?*

RH: Well, the incident that sparks the novel is true. Nat King Cole was attacked onstage by a racist mob, but this was actually in Birmingham, not Montgomery. Also, he was attacked in 1956, and I moved that moment to 1945. I thought the moment of his attack fit what happened when black veterans were attacked after World War II. I wanted to give myself a lot of space for the story since it was being told from the perspective of a fictitious driver.

I look artistic license like someone playing a radically different version of a jazz standard. It doesn't hurt the standard at all, and it may bring the standard into a conversation for those who don't know it.

TJ: *Me personally, I'm fine with playing fast and loose a little bit. You're a novelist, not a documentarian.*

RH: And I can't really see a documentary being terribly interested in the life of Cole's chauffeur, but in my novel, he's ▶

the narrator. In real life the chauffeur sees everything. He's the perfect narrator, but working-class people's stories are too often forgotten. Think about how many folks were not a part of the record. There were 50,000 black people in Montgomery during the boycott, so you think about all of those stories that are pretty much anonymous. They're part of the collective, and in fiction we're peeling characters away from that collective and giving them a voice. They had small roles, but those characters drive fiction. We can bring those anonymous folks out in a way that nonfiction can't.

TJ: *One more question. What is your favorite Nat King Cole song?*

RH: "Let's Face the Music and Dance." The first line of the song is "There may be trouble ahead."

Atlanta native Tayari Jones is the author of three novels, most recently Silver Sparrow. *She is on the MFA faculty of Rutgers-Newark University.*